A Trifling Affair
Olivia Sumner

ZEBRA BOOKS
KENSINGTON PUBLISHING CORP.

ZEBRA BOOKS

are published by

Kensington Publishing Corp.
475 Park Avenue South
New York, NY 10016

First printing: May, 1992

Printed in the United States of America

Chapter One

"Papa," Maud Hawthorn asked, "what does a girl do when her sister's the most beautiful and sought after young woman in the whole of London while she herself is plain and no one pays the slightest attention to her?"

A stout, floridly handsome man wearing his country habit of frock coat, buckskins, and top boots, Lord Ashley didn't look up from writing another number at the end of an already long row of numbers. "I suppose she raises horses and races them," he said.

"Papa! I wasn't talking about myself. I was speaking in generalities."

Her father laid his pencil down and, looking across his desk at his younger daughter, smiled fondly at her. "Whenever a young woman claims she's speaking only in generalities, the odds are eight to five she's talking about no one other than herself." He shook his head. "No, that's not right. On further consideration, I'd put those odds at better than three to one."

"But I don't raise race horses," Maud told him. "I only have Ne'er-Do-Well."

Lord Ashley looked beyond her into the past. "Did I ever tell you, Maud, how I happened to name him Ne'er-Do-Well?"

5

She tucked her feet under her on the chair. "Oh, Papa, you know very well you've told me the story many times. You called him that because you thought bettors would think twice before they wagered on a horse with such an unprepossessing name. And so his odds would be higher."

"Quite right. After you stayed up all night with him and I gave him to you as a present for helping to save his life, it was too late to change the name in the registry."

"Oh, Papa, I don't hate his name as I used to, I expect I've grown accustomed to it. But I haven't come to like mine. Maud. Take away the *u* and it becomes Mad. Take away the *a* and my name is Mud. And mud's exactly the color of my hair and eyes."

"You know why I named you Maud," her father said softly.

Dismayed by her careless words, Maud sprang from the armchair, ran around his desk, and knelt beside her father, pressing her face against his leg. She loved her father; she'd never intentionally hurt him.

"Of course I know and I'm sorry for what I said. Forgive me."

When she glanced up at the portrait by Sir Thomas Lawrence over the fireplace, the soft brown eyes of the beautiful young woman in the pale green Empire gown seemed to look reprovingly down at Maud. Her mother's picture, the rays of the May sun slanting behind her, had been painted in the springtime of her life.

Papa will grow old, Maud thought, in fact he has, but Mama never will, having died the day I was born.

Maud had never been able to bring herself to tell her father that her name had been a burden ever since she was a little girl.

"So you're Maud," Mrs. Plimsall had said one

afternoon many years before. Then, turning to her companions, she'd added in a lower yet audible voice, "Nothing at all like her poor dear mother, is she?"

The bitter memory faded as her father smoothed her hair with his hand. "Your hair's the color of her hair," he told Maud softly. "Your eyes are the color of her eyes."

"Yet Mama was beautiful just as Gweneth is beautiful. And I'm just plain Maud. My eyes are too large and my neck's too long."

"There's something I don't believe I've ever told you," her father said. "It's true I first came to Woking Manor to court your mother because she was the most breathtakingly beautiful woman I'd ever seen. But that's not why I married her. I married her because she was lively and good-hearted. Like you, Maud."

"Good-hearted! The gentlemen of the *ton* don't care a fig if one's good-hearted! Do you know what really and truly perturbs me, Papa? It's when we have a gentleman caller waiting in the Blue Room. I come to the door, and he looks up at me, expectant, and I see the hopeful light in his eyes die when he realizes it's not Gweneth but only her little sister. Will I always be the wrong sister, the wrong girl?"

"I'll make you a solemn promise, Maud. I give you my word you won't always be the wrong girl—not that you are now. Be patient. Wait a year or two and see if I'm not proved right."

A year or two! How could she bear to wait a year when a mere month seemed like an eternity? And even after a year or two nothing would change. Or would it? Wasn't anything possible? She stood up and impulsively kissed her father's cheek. "Papa, you always make me feel better. You and Ne'er-Do-Well."

"I accept the comparison with your horse for the

compliment you intended it to be," he said with a smile. "And how is he? At the top of his form for the Guildford races on Saturday week?"

Maud frowned. "I'm on my way to see him now," she said. "He was acting colicky this afternoon. I'm praying he isn't becoming sick like he did last summer."

"I was informed by one of the gamesters at Watier's that our new neighbor is entering Vulcan in the Guildford Stakes. And backing him with a heavy purse."

Maud stopped on her way to the door and turned to face her father. She was well aware the Earl of Montrain, whose ancestral home was in Cornwall, had reopened Blackstone House, some four miles to the west of Twin Oaks, after returning to England after a long sojourn in America.

"Do you mean Lord Montrain?" she asked, trying to keep her voice level.

"No other."

"I can't stand the sight of Lord Montrain. I loathe Lord Montrain."

Her father raised his eyebrows. "I didn't know you were acquainted with the gentleman. After all, he's only been back from America for a little more than four months."

"I'm not acquainted with him and I don't expect to be and I hope I never am."

"I was told Montrain's rumored to be under a cloud, something that happened while he was in the States. It happened in New Orleans, a city reputed to rival Sodom and Gomorrah combined. Or so they say at Watier's. I can't say for certain, but the difficulty or scandal or whatever it was might have involved that American who's always with him."

"His name's Philip Faurot," Maud told him.

"It's more than passing strange the way those two behave. When in public the one you call Faurot defers to Montrain but when they're alone and think they're not observed, they say 'tis the other way round. I find it especially odd since this Faurot is reputed to be as poor as a churchmouse. 'Tis as though Mr. Faurot possesses a secret hold over Montrain."

"I wouldn't be surprised, not in the least."

"It's unlike you, Maud," he said in a funning tone, "to loathe a gentleman you haven't even met."

She reddened. When would she learn to hold her tongue? She'd had no intention of telling her father what had happened a few hours before. He was too keen; he might very well be able to sense or to ferret out the fact that her opinion of Lord Montrain wasn't precisely as she'd stated it. Though that gentleman certainly *had* annoyed her.

"The scoundrel hasn't insulted you has he?" her father demanded.

She shook her head. Sighing, she realized she'd have to tell him sooner or later. "Nothing like that, Papa. Lord Montrain did worse than insult me. He ignored me."

"Failed to acknowledge you, did he?"

"Even worse than that. After I exercised Ne'er-Do-Well this afternoon I went for a walk to the glen to see if I could find any mayflowers along the brook."

She hesitated, finally deciding not to tell her father the foremost reason she went into the glen was to swing across the brook on the hanging vine she'd discovered the week before.

"On my way home," she said, "I sat leaning against the milestone on the London road to rest, and Lord Montrain and his American friend rode by. At first they must have been discussing politics, for I heard mention of Bonaparte and the Bourbons. Then they talked of tomorrow's ball at the Plimsalls'."

She paused, reliving the moment in her mind's eye, seeing them once more ride toward her, wondering what Lord Montrain would say to her, debating what her answer might be, willing herself not to be tongue-tied.

Watching him, she had to admit Gwen was right, Lord Montrain was handsome. A tall man with black curling hair, an unsmiling man, to her his deep-set eyes hinted of barely controlled passions and dark secrets. His older friend, talking with the unpleasant twang of an American, was darker and shorter. His gaze darted from side to side while he spoke, as a conspirator's might. Like Cassius, he had a lean and hungry look.

"Lord Montrain didn't ignore me," Maud told her father, "he didn't even see me. He rode past without even seeing me! As though I were some grubby child playing beside the road. And I'm only a year younger than Gwen. If I'd been Gwen, he'd not only have seen me, he'd have been off his horse in an instant offering me a ride and an escort home."

Her father sighed. "I've heard that all the young women think he's, what do they say, 'a devilishly handsome chap.' " Suddenly he frowned. "Your sister isn't taken with him, is she? Gweneth has an unfortunate proclivity for favoring completely unsuitable young men. I'm sure you remember the time she thought Georgie Plimsall would be her love for all eternity. In that case eternity turned out to last all of two months."

"Only yesterday Gwen told me she had absolutely no interest in Lord Montrain."

"A bad sign, that. When a woman says she has no interest in a man perhaps she's speaking the truth, but when she claims to have *absolutely* no interest in

10

him, I always fear the worst."

Exactly what I thought, Maud told herself, surprised her father had arrived at the same conclusion. What she said was: "Papa, don't you ever think women mean exactly what they say, no more and no less?"

Lord Ashley pondered the question. "After living all my life among women," he said at last, "and after close observation of my mother and your mother and now you and your sister, I'd have to answer you this way. Occasionally. Yes, occasionally women mean precisely what they say."

When she started to protest, her father held up his hand. "You must understand, my dear Maud, the same applies to men."

"Papa," she said, "I have absolutely no interest in Lord Montrain, and I certainly mean what I say." What prompted her to tell her father that? she wondered. The words seemed to leap unbidden to her tongue. "I'm on my way to see to Ne'er-Do-Well," she added hurriedly, thinking it best to end the conversation before her errant tongue betrayed her again.

"Is your sister about? For some reason known only to herself, she wants me to begin teaching her the rudiments of chess."

Chess? While Maud had often played with her father, her sister had never shown the slightest interest in the game. "I expect Gwen's in her room," Maud said, "still debating whether to wear her white, her mauve, or her pale green gown to the Plimsalls' ball."

"When you see her, tell her I prefer either the white or the mauve. Which will surely cause her to choose the green. Which, of course, is my actual preference."

"Papa, you're always teasing," she said, smiling when he nodded his agreement.

She loved her father and knew he returned her love

11

though he rarely put his feelings into words. What would she ever do without him? How fortunate, she thought wistfully, were those children who were loved by both a mother and a father. Who had both a mother and father to love.

She hurried to the rear hallway where she took her hooded capelet from its peg on the wall beside the door. When she settled the garment over her shoulders, she smiled ruefully, recalling the time she'd bought it — was it all of three years ago? — during her unsuccessful attempt to become more like her older sister.

How foolish she'd been then! How childishly she'd behaved! If Gwen began embroidering a runner adorned with hearts and flowers, she immediately started a runner with the same pattern. If Gwen sipped an ice as she strolled in the rose garden, she did the same. Whenever her older sister smiled, she smiled in imitation; whenever her sister frowned, she frowned.

After two months, finding she'd become no more like her sister than she'd ever been, she stopped. Yet she'd learned a lesson: one couldn't be someone else no matter how hard one tried. For better or for worse, one was fated to be oneself.

Lighting a lantern, Maud stepped into the dark night, feeling the mist dampen her face. Usually from here she could see the two rows of outbuildings behind the main house as well as something of the vista across the gardens to the grotto; but not tonight. Shivering in the unexpected chill of the May evening, she used her free hand to pull the hood over her head as she hurried toward the stables.

Ne'er-Do-Well, you will win the stakes at Guildford, Maud murmured under her breath. You won't become ill; you'll redeem yourself for last year's poor showing. And Papa will wager on you and win. And Lord Montrain will curse his luck and—

Forget Lord Montrain. Put him out of your mind.

Papa will win and be able to pay all of his debts. He doesn't think I know about the money he owes. Or about the numbers he's always writing on those long sheets of paper. They're his new method for winning at whist. Or perhaps at macao. For losing, more than likely. How proud of me he'll be when Ne'er-Do-Well outruns Vulcan from the start and wins.

Papa will hug me and tell me he'd always known we'd win. Lord Montrain will walk away with his head bowed, and then, when he doesn't think I'm looking, he'll turn to glance my way. And I'll ignore him just as he ignored me today. In fact, I'll behave as though he didn't exist. And that will surely pique his interest and—

A horse's nicker interrupted her reverie. Surprised, she raised the lantern to look around her and saw the oaks looming huge and dark in the gray mist on both sides of the drive. Behind her the light from the windows of the great house shimmered eerily; ahead of her the stables and the kennels were a little more than clusterings of shadows in the gloom. Nothing moved and the sound was not repeated.

She wondered what a horse was doing here between the house and stables, for surely no one from Twin Oaks was about on such a drear night as this. Perhaps a rider on the London road had lost his way in the fog. Or had a stableboy left a gate open? Since such carelessness was unlikely at Twin Oaks, she was confident Ne'er-Do-Well must be safe in his stall. Nevertheless she hastened her pace.

A slight movement ahead and to her right caught Maud's eye. That wasn't where she'd heard the nickering. What was it? Who was it? Something. Someone.

13

She slowed, her pulses racing, again raising the lantern to peer into the gauzy whiteness of the encompassing mist.

"Who's there?" she called.

Silence. There's naught to fear, she assured herself. It's only an animal that's wandered here from the woods, a deer or a fox. What a silly goose you are, Maud, to be frightened by every shadow, by every strange sound in the night.

But again she quickened her pace.

A twig snapped behind her. Maud's breath caught. Sensing a presence nearby, she started to turn. A hand closed over her mouth, another grasped her around the waist, pulling her back against a man's unyielding body. The lantern was yanked from her hand.

She felt herself being carried, her feet dangling above the ground. Though she twisted her head, she couldn't free herself from the hand covering her mouth. Afraid and angry, she kicked her attacker while at the same time trying to pummel him with her fists. He grunted but didn't relax his hold.

A muffled voice came from ahead of them. Again a horse nickered. She saw shadowy forms in the mist. The hand left her mouth. Just as she started to scream, someone thrust a cloth between her teeth and tied it behind her head. Hands grasped her ankles and she was swung up into a carriage seat, the sound of her racing heartbeats pounding in her ears.

A man climbed up to sit beside her, but she couldn't make out his features in the darkness. "Don't be afraid," he said in a low voice. An American voice! "You won't be harmed, I give you my word. If you'll promise not to struggle or try to run off, I'll not bind your hands or feet."

She felt the American flip the reins to urge the car-

14

riage horse forward. Another horse's muffled hoof-beats came from her right, alongside the carriage. There were at least two of them, then, the man next to her and the horseman.

"Do you promise?" The American voice again. Who else could it be but Philip Faurot, Lord Montrain's friend?

Maud nodded, replied with a strangled, "Yes."

"Good."

They rode in silence, boldly passing beside the house and along the graveled driveway, after many minutes turning from the drive onto the London road. They turned to the right toward Blackstone House, the Earl of Montrain's estate.

"I'll remove this," the American said, untying the cloth, "but I'll have to put a scarf over your eyes." He twirled the scarf, covered her eyes, and loosely knotted the ends behind her head.

The American flicked the whip, and soon the carriage was swaying from side to side as they plunged ahead at a reckless pace. Even so, Maud's panic slowly subsided. Could she believe her captor's word, believe him when he said he meant her no harm? For some reason, a reason she couldn't explain to herself, she did believe him. The American, though, she decided, was only a pawn of Lord Montrain in a deep game she didn't understand.

No, she did understand it. When her father expressed concerns about Lord Montrain's reputation, he'd told her that their newly arrived neighbor had backed his horse, Vulcan, "with a heavy purse." And now Lord Montrain meant to be certain Vulcan won the race at Guildford, that Ne'er-Do-Well's challenge would prove fruitless.

How did abducting her further Lord Montrain's nefarious plan? Perhaps he intended to keep her pris-

15

oner until after the race. But that would mean hiding her for more than a week, surely a dangerous and foolhardy undertaking. Possibly he meant to force her to reveal Ne'er-Do-Well's racing strategy. Yet this was unlikely since Ne'er-Do-Well was widely known as a front runner.

Maud shuddered with apprehension as another possibility occurred to her. Perhaps Lord Montrain and his cohort had surreptitiously made their way to the Twin Oaks stables to spirit away Ne'er-Do-Well. When she had been about to discover them at their dastardly work, they'd carried her off. Or else, and this was more likely, they were about to harm or abduct Ne'er-Do-Well only to have their scheme thwarted by her approach. Which meant they'd have to keep her prisoner long enough to allow them to return to Twin Oaks to carry out their plan.

She must escape! Even though she'd promised the American she wouldn't. To stifle her twinge of guilt, she reminded herself that all stratagems were allowed in love and war. And this was war for her as certainly as the Battle of Waterloo had been war for the Duke of Wellington.

Maud waited until they swung around a curve. She let herself sway against the side of the carriage while reaching with her hand along the edge of the seat, making certain there was no door. Good, now she'd bide her time.

The minutes dragged by as she waited, tensely expectant. At last the carriage slowed to make a sharp turn to the right. This was her chance, possibly her only chance. With her left hand she yanked off the blindfold while with her right she gripped the side of the carriage.

For a second she hesitated but then, remembering the many times she'd jumped from the swinging vine,

16

she drew in a deep breath and leaped from the moving carriage. Landing on her feet, she rolled head over heels along the grassy verge of the road.

Maud sprang to her feet, heard a man's shout, saw the full moon through wisps of fog and the overreaching limbs of trees. She ran toward the trees as hooves pounded behind her, coming closer and closer. Hands reached down and grasped her about the waist. She spun away, falling, hearing a muttered curse.

Maud pushed herself to her feet. Looking over her shoulder, she saw the rider dismount and run toward her. Lord Montrain! She ran, slowed by her long skirts. Within a few steps he overtook her and tumbled her to the ground in the shadow of the trees.

Kneeling beside her, he grasped her shoulder, turning her onto her back. His dark face loomed over her and, powerless, she trembled. When she started to scream, he leaned to her and his mouth found hers. He kissed her.

For a moment, taken by surprise and stunned by his audacity, she submitted, wide-eyed, to his kiss. For a moment longer she couldn't move, transfixed by the warmth of his lips, a warmth that swept through her, threatening to make her forget what a villain he was.

Maud twisted her face away. He stared down at her.

"Bring the lantern here," he called to his companion. "Hurry. Hurry."

She tried to free herself from his grasp and failed as she saw the pale yellow glow bobbing toward them. She'd been right. The man with the lantern was the American, Philip Faurot. She blinked in the light.

"Good God!" Lord Montrain said. "Look here, will you? We're in a deuce of a muddle. We've carried off the wrong girl!"

Chapter Two

The wrong girl! Lord Montrain's words echoed mockingly in Maud's mind. Only a short while ago she'd told her father she always turned out to be the wrong girl and now Lord Montrain seemed to confirm it.

After a long uncomfortable silence, Lord Montrain placed his hands on the ground on either side of her and pushed himself to his feet. Shaking his head as though in disappointment, he stepped back.

She sat up. As her initial surprise wore off, her growing anger brought a vivid flush to her face. How dare he do this to her!

Her hands scrabbled in the grass beside her. If only she could find a stone or a stick, she'd hurl it at him. No, she admonished herself, she mustn't give him the satisfaction of seeing her behave like a schoolgirl. She'd been brought up to be a lady, and she meant to act like one no matter how dire the provocation.

Lord Montrain, evidently determined to make the best of the muddle, swept off his hat and bowed. "My humblest apologies, Lady Maud," he said. "I abjectly beg your forgiveness for my abominable behavior. In the dark and the fog and because you were wearing that cape, I fear I mistook you for your sister."

Her sister? "Then it wasn't Ne'er-Do-Well you were after?" she asked.

"Ne'er-Do-Well? The name's dashedly familiar yet somehow I can't place it."

He appeared so puzzled she almost believed him. "Ne'er-Do-Well's my horse," she said. "I was on my way to the stable to see to him when you and your friend assaulted me. He races against Vulcan at Guildford next week."

"Oh, yes, the front runner who tires early. He's yours? I didn't know. I assure you I meant your horse no harm, especially since Vulcan has little to fear from him. Nor did I wish your sister harm. You'll forgive me, won't you, for my sad bungle, my unfortunate error?"

"Your 'unfortunate error'!" She paused, savoring the sound of the scorn she'd managed to put in her voice. "I'll never forgive you," she told him. "Never, never, never. Not just because of what you did to me, terrible as that was, but because of what you meant to do to my sister. How could you be so cruel? Did you mean to ruin her for now and forevermore?"

"The thought of ruination never entered my mind."

Since he sounded so genuinely contrite, she decided he must be a practiced deceiver. He wouldn't fool her no matter how hard he tried!

" 'Twas but a lark," he insisted. "I meant to return Lady Gweneth to Twin Oaks forthwith so no one would ever know. Except Gweneth."

"So carrying off young ladies is naught but your

19

notion of a madcap lark. Perhaps in your world it is, Lord Montrain, but it's not in mine nor Gwen's." She was so angry her words tumbled headlong one over the other. "Your wild project was dastardly, the act of a despicable coward. If you'd made off with the right girl instead of the wrong one, Gwen would never have been able to hold her head up in society again."

"Believe me, Lady Maud, I had no such intent. I'm curst sorry. I never suspected the possibility that such dire consequences might ensue. They wouldn't in America — at least not in New Orleans, though I daresay men there behave much more passionately than they do here. At times I suspect we in England are living but a pale imitation of life."

All during this exchange, Philip Faurot had been standing with the lantern in his hand and a bemused smile on his face, looking from his friend to Maud and then back again at Lord Montrain.

"I haven't the slightest notion of what they do or don't do in the American wilderness," she said, including Mr. Faurot in her glare. "Nor do I care one whit. What I do know is that I intend to tell my father what happened. I expect he'll see to it you're drummed out of London society within the fortnight."

"You'd be making a grave mistake, Lady Maud. Let me tell you why. There would always be those who'd suspect your sister wanted to be carried off; our friends and families would be forced to take sides; duels might be fought; lifelong enmities would ensue. And all because of my bit of harmless flummery."

"You should have thought of all that beforehand." She whirled away from him and started walking along the road. "And now I intend to go home."

After a few moments she became aware that Lord Montrain was following a few paces behind her. "Pray let me drive you back to Twin Oaks," he offered. " 'Tis the least I can do to make amends."

"No, I'm not interested in the least you can do nor in the most you can do. Neither's good enough for me." She walked more quickly, her shoulders stubbornly stiff and her head held high.

He walked behind her in silence for several minutes. "May I offer you a bit of advice?" he asked.

"No, you may not. I value your advice even less than I enjoy your presence, which is not at all. So kindly stop following me."

"Even without your permission, I intend to offer my advice. I do so for your own good and for my peace of mind." He paused but she said nothing. "I must warn you," he told her, in a rather self-satisfied tone she thought, "that if you intend to walk to Twin Oaks and not to Blackstone House, you're proceeding in precisely the wrong direction."

Stifling a gasp of exasperation, she stopped, realizing to her chagrin that he wasn't trying to gammon her. Taking her skirt in one hand, she turned around and swept past him without a word.

When they came once more to his carriage, a phaeton, Philip Faurot said to him, "John, I'll ride Beau back to Blackstone while you accompany Lady Maud home in the rig."

"Agreed," Lord Montrain said.

They spoke to one another as though, Maud thought, Mr. Faurot was accustomed to taking the initiative and having Lord Montrain follow his lead. Perhaps this mysterious American had had more of a hand in tonight's events than she'd suspected.

Maud walked on, wondering how far from Twin Oaks she'd been driven before she leaped from the carriage. Two or three miles, she guessed, not an impossibly long walk. Except for the patches of fog that came and went, eddying around her feet and shrouding the road. And except for the fact she hadn't put on her overshoes when leaving the house and now winced with pain each time she felt a rock or the edge of a rut through the thin soles of her slippers.

She heard hooves and the rattle of wheels behind her, and after a moment the horse, a gray mare, and the phaeton were beside her, matching her pace. From the corner of her eye she saw Lord Montrain lean down toward her.

"Please allow me to drive you home, Lady Maud," he said. "I may have acted impulsively a while ago but surely that's no crime. Don't you believe in forgiving a man's honest mistakes?"

She said nothing, averting her gaze. Perhaps, she thought, she should ride with him. After all, accepting his offer wouldn't lead him to think she condoned his actions. Besides, if she stubbornly insisted on walking all the way to Twin Oaks, her feet would be so sore tomorrow night she'd be unable to dance a step at the Plimsalls' ball. And she loved to dance.

Ready to surrender, she glanced to her left, catching her breath in surprise when she found that the phaeton was no longer there. She looked back to find Lord Montrain, reins in one hand, walking toward her leading the gray mare.

"I'll walk with you," he said when he came alongside. " 'Twill be my penance for my sin."

22

"I've decided to ride after all," she told him. "You'll have to find another way to atone."

Before she could stop him, he took her hand and led her back to the phaeton. She looked up at him in the soft glow of the moonlight—he was taller than she'd thought—telling herself she must retrieve her hand from his and yet unable to. His touch warmed her, his gaze unsettled and confused her. His eyes were dark, a deep brown she guessed, and mesmerizing.

Why was she staring at him? Why did it seem that time had stopped?

At last, his voice slightly husky, he said, "Let me help you, Lady Maud," and made haste to hand her up to the seat.

When he climbed up to sit beside her, he flipped the reins, and they were on their way. The seat was so narrow their bodies almost touched, but even though they didn't, not quite, she was distractingly aware of him. She shifted uneasily even though she didn't fear him, not exactly. All she knew was that she'd never felt this way before.

The silence between them stretched and grew taut. She wanted to break it, but she didn't trust herself not to talk foolishness since she knew she was apt to speak without thinking. She didn't want him to think her childish.

Lord Montrain cleared his throat. When he spoke, his tone, to Maud, seemed stiff and distancing, as though he realized he'd come within an ace of losing an advantage of some sort and now meant to regain it no matter what the cost.

"You probably wonder why I didn't court your sister in the usual way," he said.

When she didn't answer, he went on. "We might

compare a man's courtship of a young lady," he said, "to crossing a brook. There are many ways to get from one side of a stream to the other, just as there are many ways to proceed with a courtship. One might, for example, remove one's shoes and wade across a brook. Or one could leap from the near bank to the far bank. Or find a spot where the brook narrows and cross by stepping from one rock to the next. Yet there's still another way. One might find an overhanging vine, grasp it, and swing across the brook."

He was talking about her! Trying his best to put her at a disadvantage. She turned. "You spied on me," she accused him. "You saw me swing on the vine."

"It was by happenstance," he said, retreating in the face of her vehemence. "When I stopped at the side of the road to water my horse in the brook, the prospect so enchanted me so I followed the stream into the glen to the pool. Where, by chance, I saw you."

What must he have thought to find a young lady swinging on a vine like a denizen of the jungle, like a boy? She couldn't stop the blood from suffusing her face. His purpose in mentioning the vine was to shame her. How she hated him!

"I'll never forgive you," she told him.

"I thought the sight quite charming," he protested.

She hardly heard him. Ever since she was a child, the glen had been her secret place, her retreat from the bustle of the great house at Twin Oaks with all its guests and all its servants. Now she'd never be able to go there again without being afraid she was being spied upon.

Without warning Lord Montrain stopped the carriage. Her breath caught in surprise, and she glanced quickly at him, wondering what he intended, determined to show him that no possible conduct of his could disturb her tranquillity.

"When I travel this road," he said, "I always try to pause just here." With a sweep of his arm, he called her attention to the moonlit vista to their left.

He had stopped the carriage at the top of a slight rise. Beyond a stone wall, the western verge of the Twin Oaks estate sloped downhill to the tree-shaded brook. On the other side of the brook she saw gently rolling countryside, in the daytime a patchwork of fields where sheep and cattle grazed, now covered by a blanket of mist silvered by the moonlight. Across the valley a light glowed from the mill and from several cottages at the foot of a succession of hills, some wooded, some cleared for farming, the land rising and falling as far as the downs where clumps of trees rose like bouquets in the midst of the heather.

"Isn't it magnificent?" Lord Montrain asked her. "While I was in America, whenever my thoughts returned to England, to my homeland, as they so often did even though I'd been away many years, this is what I remembered."

Maud looked at him, surprised by his sensibility, by his love of this land, this England. On the other hand, she reminded herself, he might be deliberately trying to ingratiate himself with her by appealing to what he considered feminine susceptibilities, intending to thaw her icy hostility so she wouldn't tell her father about his dastardly crime.

As they drove on in silence, she frowned as she

25

realized that with all her heart she longed to believe in his sincerity. This perverse desire troubled and puzzled her. After what he'd done, why did she seek to make excuses for him? Whatever the reason, she promised herself she'd never let him know how confused and contradictory her feelings about him were.

When their horse and carriage pounded across the planks of the first of two bridges over the winding brook, he said, "Your secret's safe with me, Lady Maud."

Startled, wondering if he'd been able to read her innermost thoughts, she asked, "And what secret is that?"

"The pool in the glen. Your hideaway."

"Oh, the pool," she said, relieved at not being found out. "I harbor so few secrets, I suppose I treasure the ones I do have."

"You're exceptional, then, since most of us have many secrets." He seemed to be speaking as much to himself as to her. "We have more secrets than we should."

"You owe me one."

"Owe a secret? I never knew they could be owed, like money. I always thought of secrets as misdeeds we prefer to bury where no one is ever likely to unearth them."

" 'Owing a secret' is a game my sister Gwen and I played when we were young." She resisted the temptation to add, "A long, long time ago."

"Ah, I think I see what you have in mind. I chanced to discover one of your secrets, your pool in the glen, so now I owe you one of mine."

"You don't really, Lord Montrain. Only if you want to play the game."

"I fear I owe you more than a secret." He frowned, as though thinking. "If I share a secret with you, do you promise it goes no farther, that it's just between the two of us?"

"I'll not tell a living soul. That's one of the rules of the game."

"You have a bargain, then. I'll share a secret with you. Recently I've heard there's been tattle about Mr. Faurot and myself. That my friend possesses a mysterious hold over me." He looked a question at her.

"So I've been told," she said.

"This is the secret I'll share: the stories are true, after a fashion. I suppose the *ton* is convinced I committed some heinous crime in New Orleans and Faurot happened to discover my guilt and threatened to reveal it to one and all." He glanced at her from the corner of his eye, nodding when he read confirmation on her face. "Probably you suspect he became aware of my unfortunate penchant for carrying off maidens and thereby ruining their reputations."

"I never suspected anything of the kind," she said indignantly. Glancing at him, Maud saw his mouth curve in a wicked smile and realized he'd been funning her. She blushed, vowing not to be trapped into saying another word.

"No matter what you or the rest of the *beau monde* supposes, the truth is quite different. I *am* beholden to Philip Faurot and always will be. Beholden twice over because he saved my life not once but two times. You see, I was unlucky enough to serve under General Pakenham in the Battle of New Orleans, a senseless engagement fought after the war was over but before the news of the peace

27

found its way across the Atlantic to America.

"I was wounded, rather severely as a matter of fact. Philip's family happened to know the British surgeon, one Dr. McReynolds. He told the Faurots I needed more care than the army could give me in their makeshift hospital. That same day the Faurots came and brought me to their home, nursed me for several months, and as you can see I survived."

"And the other time he saved your life?"

"A duel. A hot-headed Creole challenged me to a duel with pistols. Philip's a crack shot, unluckily I'm not, so he helped me prepare for the duel. If he hadn't — "

"Did you kill the Creole?" The thought of gentlemen killing one another in affairs of "honor" dismayed her.

"No, I only succeeded in wounding the b— Pardon me, the blackguard." He reined the horse to the left and the small carriage swung onto the drive leading to Twin Oaks.

Without a doubt a woman had been the cause of the duel, Maud told herself. She imagined Lord Montrain falling desperately in love with the Creole's beautiful wife, carrying her off as he'd meant to carry off Gwen, only to have her irate husband pursue the lovers, overtake them, and challenge the Englishman.

All at once she became aware that Lord Montrain had been talking to her. "Forgive me," she said, "I didn't hear you."

" 'Favors,' " he repeated. "It's a game my brothers and I played years ago. I had three brothers and whenever we fought, my father made us play the game. I consider it only fair that the two of us play my game since I played yours by sharing my secret."

She eyed him with suspicion. "How do you play?" she asked.

"The rules are exceedingly simple." The carriage left the woods, rounded a turn in the drive, and approached the house. "But first, I had the notion you were on your way to the stables when Mr. Faurot and I happened upon you. To look after your horse? Why don't I take you there now?"

When she hesitated, he said, "Good, I'd like to see this Never-Do-Well of yours."

"Ne'er-Do-Well," she corrected him.

Stopping the phaeton in the stable yard, he leaped to the ground but, unwilling to risk another overly intimate, unsettling encounter, Maud climbed down before he could come around to help her.

Retrieving her lantern, he lit it and walked beside her into the barn, pausing just inside the door to breathe deeply. "I never tire of the aroma," he said, "of leather and hay and horses."

"I love horses," she told him. Leading him to a stall in the middle of the barn, she said, making no attempt to keep the pride from her voice, "And this is Ne'er-Do-Well."

He put his hand to his chin, studying the horse. "He's a magnificent animal." When he spoke the horse's name softly, the chestnut gelding surprised Maud by coming to Lord Montrain at once and allowing him to stroke his neck. "You have cause to be proud of him."

She noted with relief that Ne'er-Do-Well appeared fit. Her concern about his health had been groundless.

Suddenly Lord Montrain frowned. "There's a chicken in his stall," he said.

"Oh, yes, that's Little. Ne'er-Do-Well made a

29

habit of chewing on the boards of his stall until I brought the chicken to keep him company. They've become the best of friends."

Lord Montrain opened his eyes much wider than usual, then nodded.

"He's by Nonpareil out of Westwind," she went on. "The horse, not the chicken."

"Those are excellent bloodlines. I've made something of a study of the subject, at least I did many years ago before I sailed for America. Have you ever considered—?" He stopped abruptly.

"You were saying, Lord Montrain?" she prompted.

"Looking into his heritage," he finished as they walked away from the stall. "You can usually tell a great deal about a horse from his forebears. The same principle applies even more to humans."

"You may be partly right about horses, Lord Montrain, but I believe a person must be judged by what he is and does, not by the happenstance of his lineage."

"You seem to have very definite opinions."

"No, Lord Montrain," she said stiffly, "you're mistaken once again. I know not 'seems.' I *do* have very definite opinions."

"I refuse your challenge to a duel with well-honed words since even if Mr. Faurot chose to help me I could never hope to win. However, you might profit by paying more heed to meanings than to nuances." He offered her his arm. "I'll escort you to your house," he told her.

Annoyed by his rebuke, she hesitated momentarily before taking his arm. Though at first they walked along the drive in silence, she couldn't stifle her curiosity. "You mentioned a game. 'Favors,' I

30

believe you called it."

"Quite right. Whenever my brothers and I fought among ourselves, my father made us exchange favors. Not just the culprit, mind you — how can you determine who was really at fault when boys fight? — but the supposed victim as well. Since I played your game by revealing my secret, in all fairness you should take part in mine. We did fight, you and I, after a fashion."

"Your game hardly seems fair since there's no question but that you were the one at fault. You should do the favor, not both of us."

"Agreed," he said at once. "I'll do whatever you ask, and you'll not be beholden to me in the least. Pray name your favor, Lady Maud."

Afraid he'd led her into a trap, she said airily, "There's nothing you could offer that would interest me in the slightest, Lord Montrain."

"I'm sorry you've changed your mind. You might be surprised to learn I'd already hazarded a guess as to the favor you'd request."

Something had come to mind, but he couldn't possibly guess what it was. "And your guess was?"

"I expected you to ask me to dance with you at tomorrow night's ball."

She stopped to stare at him, nonplussed. "Of all the conceited, masculine, presumptuous, addle-headed, ridiculous notions. As if I cared a fig whether you danced with me or not."

"I meant to compliment you by telling you the truth, by making you privy to my thoughts rather than using high-flown falsehoods to attempt to curry favor with you. Whether you play my game or not, I'd still greatly enjoy the pleasure of dancing with you at the Plimsalls'. Will you, Lady Maud?"

31

She'd be churlish to refuse.

Especially, and this she'd never admit to a soul, since he'd been right when he'd guessed her secret wish.

"I'd be delighted, Lord Montrain," she told him. "And your favor, if I choose to grant it, would be?"

"You say I'm hopelessly inept at discovering the route to a woman's heart, so I'd be indebted for any help you might be able to give me. Tell me how best to win your sister's favor since my own attempt this evening was, as you have rightly said, misguided. Even worse than being misguided, it was bungled. Don't tell me here and now, the hour's late, but tomorrow. We could meet at the pool in the glen at five."

The gall of the man, expecting her to help him win her sister's hand! She turned to face him—they'd come to one of the rear doors of the manor—and smiled with all the sweetness and sincerity she could muster. "Until tomorrow," she murmured.

"Then you won't inform your father of tonight's unpleasantness?"

"No, I can see you're right. It would lead to no end of mischief."

He started to raise her hand to his lips but, drawing it away, she opened the door and slipped into the house.

When she paused at the window halfway up the stairs to her bedchamber, she looked down and saw his phaeton passing on the driveway below. She watched it until it disappeared beneath the trees.

"Until tomorrow," she repeated under her breath.

No, Lord Montrain, she decided, I won't tell Papa, and yes, I'll meet you at the pool. I don't know yet what I'll do to make certain you receive your comeuppance or how I'll do it, but if you expect me to help you win Gwen's heart, you're very much mistaken.

Chapter Three

Some English days are apt to bluster and rant;
many greet the wayfarer with a dampness that
chills his very bones; others lure the unwary with a
soft whisper and a charm that without warning
turns to nastiness; a few are dull and rather tedious; many manage to smile invitingly from sunrise
to sunset.

This day, this last Saturday in May in the year
1817, sang.

The sun, rising in a cloudless sky, quickly
burned off the last wisps of the morning mist.
The flowers in the gardens and fields, finding
themselves in the very heart of springtime,
bloomed riotously. Birds soared above the trees,
calling to one another, children and dogs romped
joyously, aging horses galloped with a renewed
spirit, and cats basked in the warm sun, purring
contentedly.

Of all God's creatures, only humans, as has always been their wont, welcomed the glorious day
with less than unbounded enthusiasm.

At Blackstone House, Philip Faurot rose at
dawn, saddled Caesar, and cantered across the

fields. He should, he realized, have left Blackstone and England long before, yet he lingered, postponing his departure from day to day. His dallying at Blackstone meant danger for himself, for Lord Montrain, and perhaps others as well. Yet the prize, he assured himself, was well worth the risk.

John Severn, Earl of Montrain and master of Blackstone House, breakfasted on the terrace with his mother, occasionally allowing his glance to stray eastward in the direction of Twin Oaks. He frowned as he recalled his dream of the night before in which the cowled figure of a woman had run toward him from out of the mist, stopping a few paces away and drawing back her hood. He recognized Lady Gwen Hawthorn, beautiful and remote. Suddenly Gwen was gone, and her young sister, Maud, had taken her place, smiling mischievously at him. And then Maud vanished as well, and he cried out in dismay when he found he beheld a faceless specter.

At Twin Oaks, Lord Ashley awoke with a searing pain in the large toe of his right foot. Damn the gout! And damn his debts! To add to his travails, that Frenchman, Monsieur Lusignon, was arriving that morning for an indefinite stay. He didn't like the man, didn't trust him more than half, yet the Prime Minister himself had taken Lord Ashley aside to ask him to do whatever he could to accommodate "his close friend, M. Maurice Lusignon." Lord Ashley was certain no good would come of it.

Lady Gwen Hawthorn lingered over a breakfast served in her fourposter bed. Sighing, as she was wont to do of late, she wondered how one could

35

ever be confident that another person, particularly a man, was sincere. She had so few clues to guide her: the touch of a hand, a brief, possibly inadvertent caress, the sudden light in his eyes when she entered a room, and words, endless words. Did the sum total of these things bespeak love? How could she be sure? Hadn't she been sadly mistaken many times before? Perhaps tonight at the ball she'd know.

Maud ate a hurried breakfast, ran to the stables, exercised and groomed Ne'er-Do-Well, climbed to the tower room high in the west wing, climbed down again, and talked to her father, all before eight o'clock in the morning, all in a fruitless attempt to banish Lord Montrain from her thoughts. How she hated him! At the same time, since she insisted on being absolutely honest with herself, she had to acknowledge how divided she was. Since, strange to say, she couldn't wait to see him again.

After talking to her father, Maud set off in search of Gwen, meaning to ask her which gown she intended to wear to that night's ball at the Plimsalls'. She found her sister in the library with a book open on her lap.

As Maud paused in the doorway, Gwen turned to the final page, read for a minute or two, and then snapped the cover shut. Holding the book aloft in one hand, she hurled it against the wall. The book fell with a thud onto the rose-red Axminster carpet.

"I can see you're in no mood to discuss gowns,"

Maud said as she entered the library and sat across from Gwen on the small sofa.

"The novels these days are all the same," Gwen complained. "A beautiful young lady meets a handsome, dashing, wealthy lord; we're given to understand that the fates intend them one for the other; they suffer through a series of trivial misunderstandings that could be resolved with a word or two; the predicaments are at last untangled; and they're betrothed. Finis, the tale is done."

As she listened to her sister, Maud couldn't keep images of Lord Montrain from creeping, unbidden, into her mind. "Isn't that just as it should be?" she asked. "Don't we hope the same will happen in life?"

"Fiddlesticks! *You* might imagine, little sister, that a woman's life begins with courtship and concludes with marriage, but I most assuredly don't. Marriage should be a new beginning for a woman rather than an ending. And you'll come to agree with me once you're older, at least I hope you will." She sighed. "Men might wish it otherwise, I'll grant you that."

"Yet women write most of the novels," Maud protested. "Including this one." She retrieved the book from the floor and smoothed the pages before closing it and placing it on the table.

"Those who do evidently lack minds of their own. If I were writing a novel, at the very least my final sentence wouldn't promise a betrothal. Followed by a period. And then, 'The End.'

Gwen paused, and Maud realized her sister was waiting for her to ask how she would bring her novel to its conclusion. Gwen expected her to provide accompaniment for her solo performances.

For as long as Maud could remember, she'd been perceived and, in fact, had once perceived herself as a reflection of her sister much like the moon, an orb doomed to dwell in darkness except when fortunate enough to be able to reflect the light of the sun. After all, wasn't Gweneth the older as well as the more comely of the Hawthorn sisters?

"What would you do?" Maud dutifully asked.

"If I were writing a story," Gwen used her forefinger to write imaginary words in midair, "I'd wait until I reached an intriguing part, perhaps the morning of the wedding day, and just suddenly stop. No period. No 'The End.' Merely the beginning of a sentence followed by nothing at all. To demonstrate to the reader that the heroine's life isn't over just because her wedding is in the offing."

"Wonderful." Maud clapped her hands and was rewarded by Gwen's self-satisfied smile. Maud had learned that her sister both expected and enjoyed appreciation. And, she believed, deserved it.

Suddenly an idea slithered into Maud's mind. No, that would be wrong, her conscience told her. The enticing thought must have been sent to her by the Devil himself. She'd have no part of any deception even though she had to smile when she pictured an abashed Lord Montrain receiving his comeuppance at her hands.

A comeuppance he richly deserved. She *would* do it! As long as she made certain Gwen wouldn't be hurt.

"Speaking of gentlemen and courtship and betrothals," Maud said, "Papa told me yesterday he suspected you might favor Lord Montrain." She watched her sister closely. "I told Papa nothing could be further from the truth."

For a brief moment Gwen appeared surprised and even disconcerted. Then, with a dismissive wave of her hand, she said, "As I think I told you, I met Lord Montrain and his American friend in London. Only on a very few occasions. Oh, six or seven in all, I suppose it might have been. You were quite right in telling Papa I have no interest in the Lord Montrain."

Why did she feel this sudden rush of relief? Maud wondered. For one reason only—if Gwen had been interested in Lord Montrain, she couldn't put her plan into effect, for she'd do nothing to risk her sister's happiness. No matter how much she might want to put him in his place.

"I can appreciate your lack of feeling for Lord Montrain," Maud said, "since he's haughty, rude, and overbearing. As well as unthinking and reckless." Afraid she might have given herself away, she added, "Or so I've been told."

Although Maud thought she knew her sister almost as well as she knew herself, she still asked, "What should a gentleman do if he wishes to win your favor?"

"It's not so much what he should do as what he shouldn't," Gwen said at once. "He shouldn't insist on placing me atop a pedestal since I detest being admired for attributes I inherited by the chance of birth."

Maud felt a pang as she wondered what it would be like to be admired by a man no matter

39

what the reason might be. Quickly tamping down her unseemly envy, she nodded encouragingly.

"Men are forever comparing my eyes to limpid dark pools," Gwen said. "Or declaiming on how lustrous my hair is, how alabaster my coloring, how sparkling my eyes, how entrancing my smile, or even remarking on how tiny my feet happen to be."

"How awful that must be for you." Maud wondered if her sister noticed the barb she couldn't keep from creeping into her voice.

Apparently she didn't, for Gwen went on without a pause. "If only," she said, "I could find a gentleman of the *ton* who admired me only for what I am and not what I inherited." She shook her head. "That was one of the reasons I was somewhat taken with Georgie Plimsall two years ago. Despite Georgie's many failings, he appreciated me for myself."

Maud nodded as much to herself as to Gwen. It was clear that Gwen wanted gentlemen to offer praise of her beauty along with admiration of her other qualities. What her sister wouldn't be able to abide, Maud suspected, was a beau who laid bare her many pretenses.

Which was precisely what she would encourage Lord Montrain to do by telling him how much Gwen admired men who were utterly frank.

Was she trying to be too clever by half? She didn't think so. She'd revenge herself on the overbearing Lord Montrain without harming her sister. For she loved Gwen despite her sister's vanity, despite her sister's tendency to be self-centered. After all, wasn't a queen allowed to have more faults than a mere commoner?

Gwen rose and walked to one of the high narrow windows overlooking the sweep of the driveway in front of the great house. All at once she shook her head and turned to her sister. "Maud," she said, "what a silly, vain peacock you must think me. My only excuse is my mind's in such a dither these days. I'm so addled. Please don't hate me, Maud. Can I help it if I'm afraid?"

She couldn't credit what she'd heard. "Afraid?"

"Of leaving Twin Oaks when I marry, of leaving Papa and you. Of making a mistake."

Maud ran to her sister and hugged her. "Oh, Gwen," she said, "how could I ever hate you? I love you."

"You're all I have, little sister. Except Papa, of course, but he's old and wouldn't understand. And our Mrs. Wilcomb is decidedly superannuated. Did you know that sometimes I wish I were your age again, Maud, and didn't have to wonder whether men were sincere, whether they would keep all of their promises."

At least, Maud thought wistfully, they paid Gwen compliments, whether they were sincere or not. Wasn't that better than being ignored? She asked, "Is it one man in particular?"

Gwen hesitated so long that Maud began to suspect her sister had a secret, a secret she longed to share but for some reason couldn't.

Finally Gwen frowned and shook her head. "All men in general," she said, "no one of them in particular."

Maud, realizing the moment for shared confidences had passed, felt troubled. Gwen had freely confided in her when she'd been taken with Georgie Plimsall and with young Atherton, why didn't she now? After a pause, Maud said, "I came looking for you to ask which gown you intend to wear to the ball."

"The green. I know Papa wants me to wear it, and so I will. I suppose the gown reminds him of her. Of Mama." She shook her head sadly. "What do you think she was like? I know Papa tries to tell us but was she actually as he remembers her?"

"I daresay Mama was something like you," Maud said, "since there's no doubt she looked like you. And perhaps she was a bit like me. But mostly like herself. Do you remember her at all?"

Gwen sighed. "I wish I did, but I've tried and tried to recall what she was like to no avail."

A horn sounded from outside the house, and when they looked from the window, they saw a large coach emerge from the trees and swing around the drive toward the steps leading to the front entrance of Twin Oaks.

"A Napoleon carriage," Gwen said with a touch of awe in her voice. "Isn't it magnificent?"

Maud nodded. The elegant coach, a miniature movable palace drawn by four black horses was, indeed, magnificent from its polished brass fittings to its doors adorned with a red, green, and gilt coat of arms. Even before the carriage stopped, one of the two liveried footman sprang to ground, ran to lower the steps and, with a sweeping bow, swung open the door.

The gentleman who presently emerged was dressed in black from his top hat to his narrow, pointed shoes. A tall slender man proudly displaying a thin black moustache, he had an aquiline nose and the darkest, most deep-set eyes Maud had ever seen. While not handsome by conventional standards, he was, she thought, a man one turned to look at a second time.

"M. Maurice Lusignon," Maud whispered, "Papa told me he would arrive today."

M. Lusignon paused at the foot of the stone steps. Tucking his cane under his arm, he rubbed his gloved hands together in what appeared to Maud to be a self-satisfied gesture. Although he looked straight ahead, his eyes flicked from side to side as though he anticipated an ambuscade. Apparently having assured himself that no enemies lay in wait, he trotted up the steps and out of sight.

Maud saw her sister shiver. "I know no reason," Gwen said, "but I'm cold. As though clouds suddenly covered the sun." She reached out, took Maud's hand in hers, and when Maud returned the pressure of her fingers, Gwen smiled, apparently reassured.

Five o'clock. He *had* told her five. She'd repeated the time so often she was confident almost to the point of being uncertain. Not four, not six, he'd said five. Still, determined to arrive at the pool on time, Maud had Agnes help her put on her serviceable high-waisted white muslin and, wearing her red and white checked bonnet, left the house a half-hour early.

She was on her way, unaccompanied, to a rendezvous with a stranger. Quite disgraceful! Yet if anyone discovered that she'd been abducted the night before, she'd be ruined anyway. In for one

43

ruination, she decided, in for a pair. Besides, Lord Montrain considered her a child rather than a young lady. He did, didn't he?

She ran past the stables and into the woods, slowed to a walk to climb the hill, ran again when she came to the path leading down from the crest into the shadows of the glen. The murmur of the brook far below made her heart race in anticipation.

When she saw Lord Montrain's horse, Beau, tethered on the other side of the brook, she again slowed to a walk, drawing in deep breaths to compose herself, not wanting him to think she'd run all the way from the house. As a schoolgirl might. As a young lady raised in a genteel way never would.

Then, looking down through the new-green leaves, she saw Lord Montrain standing by the far side of the pool dressed in gray. His hat, frock coat, breeches were all gray. She stopped to watch him, the fact that he was unaware of her presence giving Maud a sense of secretly sampling forbidden fruit.

As she watched, he removed his frock coat, folded it with care, and placed it on the grass. Maud frowned in puzzlement. What was he about? Lord Montrain walked to the top of the knoll, her knoll, and glanced around the glen, evidently to satisfy himself he wasn't being observed, then grasped the vine hanging from one of the trees.

Maud drew in her breath in surprise. He yanked several times on the vine, testing it. She smiled. He ran, holding the vine with both hands, and swung out over the pool. Her hand went to her mouth to suppress a giggle. He let go of the vine, dropping to the ground on her side of the brook.

She hastily retreated back up the path, so he wouldn't catch sight of her.

When next she looked, he was leaping from rock to rock to recross the brook. Good heavens, she told herself, he was acting just like a small boy at play! Could it be that men were merely overgrown boys? She'd never thought of them in quite that way, but evidently it was true.

She reviewed in her mind how the gentlemen of the *ton* disported themselves. They played games — cards, dice, and the racing of horses; they fought one another — duels and war; they organized and joined clubs and societies — White's and Watier's and all the rest. Their pursuits were essentially the same whether they were ten years old or thirty.

Maud examined the implications of her discovery. She'd always been at ease with boys — as often as not they considered her to be one of them. Men, on the other hand, she tended to hold in awe. How foolish! They were nothing more than boys grown a tad older, perhaps a bit more cynical, and definitely more high-nosed.

She walked boldly down the path to find Lord Montrain buttoning his frock coat. When he saw her he smiled, crossed the brook once more, stepping from rock to rock rather than propelling himself through the air on the vine, and greeted her by bowing over her hand. He might be nothing more than an overgrown boy, Maud told herself, yet no boy's touch had ever made her feel so confused, so at sea, so all atingle.

45

He brushed off the top of a flat rock; he spread a dark blue handkerchief over it; he invited her to be seated. She sat, lacing her hands primly in her lap.

"Your sister," he prompted. "You were to tell me of Lady Gwen's predilections."

Maud started to speak, stopped, started once again, stopped a second time. No, she couldn't prevaricate. Gwen wasn't as uninterested in Lord Montrain as she professed to be. Maud had deluded herself into believing in her sister's indifference. For all she knew, he could be Gwen's secret. Suddenly all of the falsehoods she had so carefully rehearsed fell away, and she found herself telling him the truth as best she could even though each word she spoke added another burden to weigh on her already heavy heart.

When she was done, he nodded gravely and said, "I thank you, Lady Maud."

"I suspect you might have a rival," she couldn't help adding. She was determined to discomfit him in some manner, no matter how insignificant.

"A rival?" Lord Montrain raised one eyebrow in mock concern.

"A Frenchman."

This revelation caused him to become, if she read him aright, genuinely agitated. Abandoning his pose of indifference, he said, "Tell me about this Frenchman."

"I don't know if he's actually your rival," she confessed, "though he could well be, and he *is* staying at Twin Oaks for the next few weeks or even longer. M. Maurice Lusignon is his name."

"My God." Lord Montrain swung away from

her, so she was able to catch only a glimmering of the consternation the name had caused him.

"He's not nearly as handsome as you," she assured him. Why had she said that? she wondered.

When he turned to her his lips were curved in a faint, false smile that told her he was still perturbed. "Weren't you ever instructed," he asked, "not to utter the first thought that enters your head?"

"Ah, that's one lesson I failed to master. There were many others, Mrs. Wilcomb always said." When she saw his questioning look, she added, "Mrs. Wilcomb's a distant cousin of my father who served as our governess."

"The older we become," he told her, "the more pretenses we're forced to adopt, the more masks we wear until, if we don't take care, we become completely artificial creatures." All at once he knelt before her. "Pray don't change, Lady Maud," he said, taking her hand. "Pray remain exactly the way you are."

She snatched her hand away. Did he consider her a child? Was he telling her to remain a child? Sensing telltale tears gathering in her eyes, she stood and fled, crossing the brook and running up the path leading from the glen. When she came to the trees and looked back over her shoulder, he was still kneeling, his head bowed.

She'd sacrificed her own happiness for her sister, she reminded herself. She'd behaved nobly in guiding Lord Montrain onto the path that would allow him to win Gwen's affections. Why, then, were tears coursing down her cheeks? Why, then, did she feel so hollow, so empty, so terribly broken-hearted?

If she had been able to overhear a conversation between Lord Montrain and his friend, Philip Faurot, a few hours later as those two gentlemen drove in the Blackstone barouche to the Plimsalls' ball, her perturbation would undoubtedly have been even greater . . .

Philip Faurot removed a gold snuffbox from his pocket, opened it, and took a pinch of snuff.

"They'll suspect you're not an American," Lord Montrain told him, "if they see you inhaling snuff."

"Must I learn to chew tobacco to be thought an American? Everyone knows I'm from New Orleans which is one of the most cosmopolitan cities in the world." He glanced at his companion. "Are you becoming uneasy, John?"

"I'll admit I don't like this deviousness," Montrain said, "not one bit. If we're not careful, we're apt to end up in a deuce of a coil."

"My friend, this isn't like you. It's my neck at risk; let me be the one to worry about preserving it."

"You misunderstand, Philip. It's not you I'm concerned about: you're quite able to look after yourself. It's our cozening the Hawthorn sisters I find repugnant. Especially now that your Maurice Lusignon has put in an appearance. Not only is he here in Surrey, he's a guest in their house. How long will it be before he gets wind of the lay of the land?"

"He knows naught. He's fishing for information, nothing more. He may suspect the truth, but until he knows for certain he can do nothing."

"We should have been on our way to France long ago," Lord Montrain said.

"What is your English expression? Love conquers all?" Philip smiled. "Do I detect a *tendre* on your part for this girl, this Maud Hawthorn?"

"Don't be a gudgeon."

"A gudgeon? My dear Montrain, why don't you English learn to speak without using this abominable slang of yours?"

"For your information, my dear Faurot, a gudgeon is a perfectly respectable word. It happens to be a small fish ofttimes used for bait. Ergo, a man's a gudgeon when he's being used, when he's a dupe, or when he's in error."

"I notice you've defined a word for my benefit without speaking to the issue at hand."

"You refer, I suppose, to Lady Maud Hawthorn. She's a mere chit of a schoolgirl. I can object to our lying and pretending without having a partiality for our victim."

"Though I don't accept your description of Lady Maud, my friend, if I'm mistaken about your partiality, I apologize. Think of this as a chess game. We made our opening move, and now M. Lusignon has countered by taking up residence at Twin Oaks."

"And Lady Maud and Lady Gwen are mere pawns?"

"Not at all. They're much more important than that — at least one of them is." He leaned forward. "Look, I see the lights of the Plimsall house and

49

the carriages and your fellow Englishmen and their ladies arrayed in all their finery. Listen to that delightful music. We've arrived at the ball, so let the game continue."

Chapter Four

"These country balls are so apt to be tiresome," Gwen complained, "once you've become accustomed to the parties at Almack's. It's unfortunate, but they can't help but have a decidedly lower tone."

How Maud wished her sister didn't insist on being so high in the instep. "I've no doubt," she said, "that we still have time to ask Papa to turn the carriage around so Walters can drive you back to Twin Oaks."

Maud hadn't managed to keep the tart edge from her voice, since only a short while before Gwen had been all aflutter as they dressed for the ball. Her older sister had attempted to conceal the symptoms—namely a bright gleam in her eyes and an eager lilt to her voice—but Maud's practiced eye and ear had noted them without being able to fathom whether the cause was the prospect of dancing at the Plimsalls' or something else entirely.

"There's always that marvelous Plimsall staircase to look forward to," old Mrs. Wilcomb offered.

"Possibly," Gwen said, "there are a goodly number of ladies and gentlemen in Surrey who attend the Plimsalls' ball to admire their staircase, but I

51

don't happen to be among them."

"In all probability Lord Montrain will be at the ball." Maud made the prediction knowing full well he would be.

"Lord Montrain may have had a devastating effect upon the ladies of the *ton,*" Gwen said, "but his presence at the Plimsalls' is a matter of complete and utter indifference to me."

Lord Ashley cleared his throat. "It's been my observation," he said, "that we often belittle something when our hopes for it are unusually high. To ward off being overly disappointed, I expect."

Maud gave her father a sharp glance. He often seemed to pay little heed to what went on around him only to surprise everyone with a telling comment.

"Their staircase never disappoints me," Mrs. Wilcomb said with blithe irrelevance. "If I'm ever fortunate enough to have a house of my own, I'd like to have one like it. On a much more modest scale, for course. I only regret M. Lusignon was so fatigued by his journey to Twin Oaks that he'll miss this chance to see it."

"To my way of thinking," Maud said, "it's more like magic." When she saw all three of her companions turn to her with puzzlement in their eyes, she did her best to explain. "Not the staircase. I refer to the belittling. I suppose we've all learned the fates are usually perverse, so when we say we expect nothing we hope they'll do their very best to prove us wrong."

She didn't expect to be disappointed tonight. No, she was absolutely certain she would be. After returning home from the glen she'd decided to accept her dreary fate and face life with an air of noble resignation.

Closing her eyes, she pictured a contrite Lord Montrain coming to her in the far distant future, kneeling at her side, taking her hand in his, and murmuring, "My dear Maud, I have a confession to make. I've known for many years that you were the one I should have offered for, not your sister Gweneth."

Maud sighed a sigh of bittersweet satisfaction . . .

Her father's chiding voice brought her thoughts back to the present. "If you don't rouse from your reverie, miss," he told her, "you'll be the one returned to Twin Oaks, not your sister."

She opened her eyes to find they had arrived at the Plimsalls'.

A visitor entering Plimsall Manor was immediately confronted by the great staircase. The Plimsall who built the house in 1733 copied the design of the staircase from one he'd seen in a Florentine palace during a tour of Italy several years before. He proceeded to import the required tons of white Carrara marble, the same variety used by the sculptor Michelangelo, he boasted, an undertaking so expensive that he was forced to skimp on the remainder of the house. While the Plimsall staircase was indeed magnificent, the house to which it served as an introduction was decidedly second rate.

The Plimsalls themselves, or so several less than kind observers maintained, reflected this same inconsistency. They possessed a certain flair of a very limited scope but unfortunately, all in all,

53

they were invariably below standard. Which was why Lord Ashley had been so perturbed by Gwen's sudden favoring of young Georgie Plimsall. Georgie's flair was clothes, particularly cravats; he was often referred to as "the second Beau Brummell."

Lord Ashley's party mounted the steps slowly, pausing now and again so Mrs. Wilcomb could both catch her breath and admire the staircase. Not only were the stairs made of Carrara marble, the imposing balustrades were fashioned from the same material. Spaced at regular intervals atop these balustrades were candelabras, each holding nine glowing candles.

Mr. Robert Plimsall greeted Lord Ashley's party at the stair's summit. The elder Mr. Plimsall's specialty happened to be collecting enameled snuffboxes, possessing, at his most recent reckoning, eight hundred and thirty-six different varieties. "So much for Beau Brummell," Robert Plimsall was fond of saying, since Mr. Brummell had reputedly owned only three hundred and sixty-five snuffboxes, a different one for each day of the year.

Young Georgie Plimsall was nowhere in view but his wife, Elvira, smiled cheerfully at her arriving guests. The mother of a not quite year-old male Plimsall, she was once again in the family way. This circumstance had led Lord Ashley to observe at Watier's that Georgie, of all the Plimsalls, evidently possessed not one but two talents.

Maud stood on tiptoe to look across the ballroom floor, her heart giving a tug when she saw Lord Montrain in a green dress coat and satin knee breeches of a lighter shade of the same color.

At first she didn't see his friend, Philip Faurot, but eventually espied him in an alcove talking to Lord Montrain's mother and Mrs. Comfort, an attractive though no longer young widow.

Maud was soon claimed by Rob Atherton for a set of country dances. She never lacked for partners to lead her out onto the floor at Surrey dances, she thought with a rueful smile. Since she'd been a companion of most of the local young men since early childhood, they considered her to be one of their own and so invariably sought her out in lieu of the more sophisticated and therefore more daunting young women.

Usually she was caught up at once in the exhilarating swirl of music and the whirling gaiety of the dance. Not tonight. Time and time again she found her gaze and her attention wandering from her partner and the other dancers to the adjoining sitting room where Gwen held court for a sizeable coterie of admirers.

She'd never seen her sister look more dazzling. Gwen's willow green Indian muslin gown with a silver ribbon at the waist and silver-edged ruffles at the bodice modestly called attention to her slender yet attractively curved figure. Her face glowed in the candlelight from the two tiered chandeliers while her brown ringlets were crowned by a silver diadem studded with a constellation of jeweled stars.

". . . seem a thousand miles away."

Realizing Rob had spoken to her, Maud looked away from her sister to gaze guiltily at her partner.

"I asked what you thought of Ne'er-Do-Well's

55

chances in next week's race at Guildford," Rob said.

"He's fit. He'll do his very best," she said before the dance took her away from Rob.

By the time she located Gwen once more, her sister was walking toward the dance floor. Maud caught her breath. Only Lord Montrain was with her now. All of Gwen's other admirers had been left standing in a disgruntled, envious cluster.

Lord Montrain was talking earnestly while Gwen appeared unmoved. Lord Montrain gestured with his hand to her gown, to her face, to her hair. He must be complimenting her just as Maud had advised him to do. Gwen smiled politely. Could it be, Maud wondered hopefully, that her sister didn't find him appealing?

In response to something he said, Gwen gave a slight gasp. Raising her fan to her face, she looked past him to the French doors leading onto the terrace. After a long moment she nodded.

Now Lord Montrain talked rapidly, a faint smile on his lips. Gwen listened with her gaze fixed on him, a rapt look on her face. Maud sighed, resigned to the inevitable. How handsome he was, she thought, how poised, how urbane. She could imagine what he was telling her sister. Hadn't Maud herself suggested the topics if not the actual words?

"Beauty, though," she imagined him saying in his low vibrant voice, "is but skin deep and of the moment. True beauty, and you possess true beauty, Lady Gwen, springs from the mind and from the heart rather than from the features. And true beauty is everlasting."

By closing her eyes, Maud could almost picture him saying the words to her rather than to Gwen. "Ooof!"

Maud's eyes flew open. She found Charles Headley facing her with his hands clutching his stomach and a look of distressed surprise on his face. She realized that somehow her errant elbow had struck him a solid blow.

"Oh, Charles," she told him, "I'm so sorry, I must have been woolgathering."

As he nodded his acceptance of her apology, she became aware that the music had stopped. She fled from the dance floor. What was the matter with her? she wondered. She could never remember behaving in such an addled way before.

"Lady Maud." She frowned as she sought to identify the slightly accented voice coming from behind her. Turning slowly, she tried not to stare since at first she failed to recognize the man in gray.

"M. Lusignon," she said at last. When she'd watched him arrive at Twin Oaks and when she'd been introduced to him a short while later in the drawing room, he'd been dour and preoccupied. Now he smiled charmingly at her.

A bit flustered by the obvious admiration in his eyes, she said, "How fortunate you were able to come to the ball, after all."

"Ah," he said, "a Frenchman is never too fatigued to dance with a lovely young woman. May I have the honor?" He offered her his arm.

Taken by surprise, she could only nod her assent. When they took their places for the set, she noticed Rob Atherton, Charles Headley, and the other young men casting speculative glances at her and her new partner. Maud raised her chin defiantly. They might still consider her a girl, but she wasn't, she was a young lady. To M. Lusignon at least.

The music began. Gwen, she noted with a twinge of envy, was dancing with Lord Montrain.

"Your sister, Lady Gweneth," M. Lusignon said when the dance brought them together for a few moments, "is *très belle,* very beautiful."

Accustomed to hearing men praise her sister, she merely nodded her agreement.

"Like a marvelous painting by your Sir Joshua Reynolds," M. Lusignon went on, "to hang on one's wall to admire at one's leisure. Or like a rose plucked at full bloom from the garden of M. Plimsall. You have undoubtedly noticed, Lady Maud, the fact that many men are attracted to flowers in bloom. There are other connoisseurs of beauty, however, and I must confess I include myself among them, who much prefer the bud to the bloom."

He looked at Maud intently, making her aware he possessed a rare ability. He was capable of devoting his complete and undivided attention to his partner, making her feel the two of them were alone rather than merely one couple among many.

"There are those," he murmured so only she could hear, "who enjoy watching the unfolding, who appreciate that wonderful and priceless moment when the bud at last awakens to achieve its destiny by becoming a magnificent flower."

The whirl of the dance parted them. She was stirred by M. Lusignon's words and by his flattering attention but mostly by the envious looks she was attracting from the other women and the reappraising glances from the men. At the same time she couldn't suppress a smile as she pictured the elegant Frenchman pursuing her amidst the shrubbery of the Plimsall garden brandishing a pair of shears in his hand.

When the set of dances ended with a quadrille, M. Lusignon brought her a glass of iced champagne. She raised the drink to her lips, pausing before taking her first sip to enjoy the tingle of the bursting bubbles in her nose. Looking past an obviously amused M. Lusignon, she saw Lord Montrain escort Gwen from the ballroom onto the terrace beyond.

"Shall we sample the night air as well as the champagne?" M. Lusignon asked.

Lightheaded after only a few sips of the wine, she nodded as she put her glass down, believing the cool air would clear her head. Accepting his arm, she let him lead her across the ballroom.

She caught a glimpse of her father standing, drink in hand, regaling a group of cronies with a story. If not about racing, then certainly about shooting, hunting, or dining. Mrs. Wilcomb sat in one of the alcoves with several older women, all dressed in black, their heads inclined toward one another as, she imagined, they reminisced about other times and other balls.

As Maud accompanied M. Lusignon across the flagstones of the terrace to the top of the steps leading to the garden, she breathed in the sweet scent of roses. Heaven must, she thought, have an aroma such as this.

59

"You look enchanting, my dear," M. Lusignon told her. "So young, so eager for life, yet as pure and innocent as your white gown."

She wondered if his compliments were merely perfunctory—after all, he was French—or sincere. Whatever his intent might be, his words caused her to experience a vague unease. Though she *was* wearing a new dress, she considered it simple and rather elegant rather than innocent, a white gown with a jonquil yellow ribbon at the high waist and other ribbons of the same color threaded through the wide frill on the hem. Her ribbon bandeau, also yellow, was tastefully decorated with artificial roses.

They walked down the steps and strolled, her hand lightly on his arm, along a path illuminated by lanterns hanging from wires strung between the trees. It resembled a miniature Vauxhall Gardens, Maud thought.

"Perhaps," M. Lusignon said, "you might assist me in solving a small puzzle."

"If I possibly can," she told him.

"The puzzle concerns M. Plimsall the younger. When I arrived here this evening, regrettably rather late, he greeted me at the top of his ridiculously grandiose staircase wearing a crimson cravat. That I did not find remarkable in the least. Later in the evening, however, I encountered this same gentleman adorned with a neckpiece of a different color and tied in a somewhat different fashion. An accident had occurred, I told myself, and his cravat had suffered a stain. Then, still later, I met M. Plimsall wearing yet another cravat tied even more elaborately. This I could not explain; this is the small puzzle."

She laughed. "You may see him again later this evening wearing still another cravat knotted in yet another style. Cravats are Georgie's avocation. He has hundreds of them and is able to tie them in twenty-nine different ways. Or is it thirty-nine ways? I've quite forgotten."

"How very strange." M. Lusignon frowned and shook his head. "Can it be that M. Plimsall and the fops and dandies I meet in London are some of the same young Englishmen who defeated the great Napoleon at Waterloo?"

Maud held her head a bit higher. "Perhaps there's more to the English, sir, than your philosophy allows for," she told him proudly. Thinking of Lord Montrain fighting and suffering a wound in the Battle of New Orleans, she said, "Perhaps Englishmen can be both warriors and gentlemen. Perhaps—"

She hesitated, her breath catching as she recognized Gwen's silhouette in the shadows a short distance ahead of them. Her sister was looking raptly up at a man who stood in complete darkness, and as Maud stopped, dismayed, Gwen lifted her face to kiss him.

Maud shivered. "I'm afraid I'm frightfully cold," she said, turning and walking quickly back toward the house. She didn't think M. Lusignon had recognized Gwen, certainly she hoped not. All at once the scent of the roses seemed cloying, suffocating.

"My apologies," M. Lusignon said, "I should have thought to bring your shawl." After a pause, he went on. "I grant you the English may have

61

two sides to their character. It's possible, for instance, that your sister, the Lady Gweneth, is both a lady of great dignity and also somewhat of an adventuress."

So he had seen Gwen!

"And what about yourself, Lady Maud, are you both the young innocent you want us all to believe you are and yet also a free spirit anxious to try her wings in the great world?"

"I fear I'm only what I appear to be," she told him as they climbed the steps to the terrace. "If I tried my wings I'm afraid I'd fly, as we English say, directly from the frying pan into the fire." She stopped at the top of the steps to face him. "And what of you, M. Lusignon? What secret self are you concealing?"

He raised his eyebrows in mock dismay in response to her challenge. "Ah, Lady Maud," he said, "this is neither the time nor the place for revelations of our secret selves." He glanced toward the door to the ballroom where Henry Summerton was bearing down on them to claim Maud for a promised dance. "I suspect," M. Lusignon said, "we'll meet another day for a tête-à-tête and we'll exchange secrets then, you and I."

Later, as Maud sat beside Mrs. Wilcomb watching the dancers, she felt anger at Lord Montrain simmering within her. He'd used her help to insinuate himself into Gwen's affections, and now he risked embarrassing Gwen in front of all her friends by kissing her in what was almost a public place. When next they met she meant to tell him exactly what an abominable person he was.

"Lady Maud."

Looking up, she blinked when she found Lord Montrain towering over her.

"Lady Maud—" he began again.

She stood abruptly. "Pray don't utter another word." She had to raise her voice to be heard over the music and the murmur of talk. "Do you mean to disgrace us all?" she demanded. "Are you engaged in a vendetta of some sort against the Hawthorn?"

He stepped back, his eyes narrowing as he stared at her. Slowly a sardonic smile curled his lips. He had such an infuriating smile! "Although I've come to expect the unexpected from you," he began, "I don't think—"

"Precisely. You've scored a hit, a palpable hit. You don't think, my dear Lord Montrain. You should start to practice that activity as soon as possible although I harbor doubts as to your capabilities. Tonight you set out to ruin Gwen just as two days ago"—at this moment the music stopped, and in the sudden silence, her angry voice carried to the far corners of the ballroom—"you did your best to ruin me."

Maud's hand flew to her mouth when she realized that all around her people were staring, the women open-mouthed, the men studying her through their quizzing glasses. She turned from Lord Montrain and fled from the room to the terrace, then ran down the steps into the garden where she stumbled into the semidarkness until she discovered a stone bench to sit on. She lowered her head as tears welled in her eyes. She'd disgraced herself. What could she have been thinking of to say such a thing?

"Ahem." She looked up to see who had cleared his throat.

"You!" was all she could manage to say.

Lord Montrain said, "I admit it is I." He sat beside her, took his handkerchief, and dabbed at the tears on her face. "It's all right, Maud," he said.

Her heart lifted. Not Lady Maud, he'd called her Maud. She should resent the familiarity, but instead it warmed her.

"I explained your fit of pique to everyone's satisfaction," he told her. "I admitted I'd promised to dance with you and it had completely slipped my mind. Naturally you had cause to be distressed and reason to express your unhappiness."

How insufferable the man was to imagine she'd be that perturbed by his forgetfulness. Yet anyone who knew him would believe his story. "Then I'm not ruined after all?" she asked.

"Not in the least, I assure you. And now, if you'll but honor me with the pleasure of our forgotten dance, the whole world will see we're reconciled."

She hesitated only an instant before giving him her hand and allowing him to lead her from the garden to the terrace. I must dance with him, she thought, refusing to admit to herself how much she wanted to, for if I don't everyone will wonder why.

She heard the lilting strains of a waltz coming from the open door to the ballroom. This isn't London, she told herself. Surely it's not improper for me to dance a waltz here in Surrey.

When she nodded, he took her in his arms and

together they danced across the flagstones, through the door, and into the ballroom.

Her anger dissolved in a thrice. She felt light as a feather as if a great weight had been removed. Lord Montrain had redeemed himself in her eyes. She forgave him everything. At least for now.

Dancing with him, she lost all sense of the passing of time, all sense of where she was. As she responded to his slightest touch, she didn't dance but flew on the soaring wings of song. The two of them, in one another's arms, whirled across a celestial ballroom lit by hundreds upon hundreds of twinkling stars. They were alone together, this waltz would never end, and she and Lord Montrain were destined to dance through all eternity.

Chapter Five

On the morning after the ball, Maud hurried to the library directly after breakfast. Pushing her father's book ladder into position, she climbed to the fourth step so she could read the titles of the books on the next to the top shelf.

"I thought that's where it was," she murmured to herself.

She slid *Roman Mythology Illustrated* from the shelf, climbed down the ladder, and carried the book to the table where she sat down and opened it to the index. Running her finger down the listings, she found Icarus, turned to the indicated page, and began to read.

She discovered the story was much as she'd remembered it. Icarus and his father, Daedalus, had been imprisoned in the labyrinth on the Mediterranean island of Crete. Daedalus, an architect and an exceedingly clever man, on finding their escape thwarted by land and by sea, devised pairs of wings for both himself and his son.

"Be careful not to approach too near the sun," Daedalus warned the boy as they flew from the labyrinth and out over the sea. The young and impetuous Icarus, however, euphoric because he had escaped captivity and thrilled by being able to fly, ignored his father's warning, soaring higher and higher until the heat of the sun melted his wax wings and he plummeted to his death in the Mediterranean.

Maud sighed as she closed the book. Last night, she thought, I was the one who flew too high. I didn't heed the warnings of my mind; rather, I allowed my foolish heart to lead me astray. When I waltzed with Lord Montrain, I approached too near to the sun and now, this morning, I've come plummeting down. Not into the sea like Icarus; rather, I've fallen back to earth.

Do I actually mean to equate Lord Montrain with the sun? she asked herself. If he could somehow divine my thoughts, though, he wouldn't be the least bit surprised by the comparison; in fact he'd consider it only his due. He's vain, he's egotistical, he's nowhere nearly as handsome as he imagines himself to be. He must have some redeeming features, but I can't think of one. Gwen is certainly welcome to him.

Closing her eyes, Maud fell into a reverie, picturing herself standing alone in front of the pier glass in her bedchamber wearing a bridesmaid's gown of ruffled pink silk. She imagined she heard a tapping at the door . . .

"Come in," she said, expecting to see Gwen, the bride-to-be.

The door swung open and she gasped as Lord Montrain strode across the room to kneel at her feet. Before she could protest this blatant flouting of propriety, he grasped her hand. "Maud, my dearest," he said, "I pray I haven't waited too long before approaching you. Only at this late hour have I at last come to realize it's you I love, not your sister Gweneth. Come, my darling Maud, fly with me to Gretna Green."

Slowly, sadly, she removed her hand from his. "Oh, John," she murmured, "I cannot elope with you. The time for you to declare yourself came and went many months ago. Poor dear Gwen could never survive the disgrace of being abandoned at the altar nor the heartbreak of losing her beloved to her younger sister. No matter what our feelings may be, we must consider her happiness, not ours."

"Even before I spoke," he told her, "I knew my plea was doomed to be rejected. You, dearest Maud, are true to your loved ones. All in all you're the kindest, most tenderhearted person I have ever known or ever hope to know. These self-same wonderful qualities that have brought me — albeit, to my everlasting regret, belatedly — to love you now force you to spurn my offer of marriage. All that is left for the two of us, my dearest Maud, is to — "

A rapping made Maud's eyes spring open. For an instant she thought it must be Lord Montrain at the library door. No, that had been in her imaginings.

Glancing across the book room, she saw Gwen in the doorway tapping the crook of her parasol against the frame. Her sister, looking beguilingly trim even in her rather drab brown traveling gown, shook her head.

"Dear Maud," Gwen said in a long-suffering tone, "I suspect that with your daydreaming you've quite forgotten about me."

Maud gasped. She *had* forgotten. Gwen was leaving that morning to spend the next few days with the Harcourt twins, Floranne and Doranne, at their estate near Epsom. After joining Lord Ashley and Maud at the Guildford races she'd return to Twin Oaks with them.

She ran to Gwen and hugged her. "Forgive me, sister, but it did slip my mind. Has the Harcourt traveling chaise arrived?"

"Not as yet. We expect it at any moment."

They walked with arms entwined into the green drawing room where they sat side by side on the settee.

"Have you changed your opinion of Lord Montrain?" Maud asked, glancing sideways to gauge any telltale nuance in her sister's response.

"Lord Montrain's an exceedingly graceful dancer and an engaging conversationalist." Gwen's expression offered no clue to her feelings.

Maud gave an inaudible sigh. Many people, she'd observed, particularly members of her own sex, Gwen included, possessed an ability to answer a question in what appeared at first hearing to be a forthcoming manner. When, however, the answer was subjected to even a superficial scrutiny, the questioner discovered that nothing whatsoever of substance had been revealed.

"Last evening most assuredly held its share of surprises," Gwen went on. "Our guest, M. Lusignon, for instance, appeared to be quite taken with a certain Lady Maud Hawthorn. Or should I say *mademoiselle?* It goes without saying that his attentions to you inspired considerable behind-the-fans chat."

"Our visitor from France is an exceedingly grace-ful dancer and an engaging conversationalist."

Gwen gave her sister a speaking look, then put her head back and laughed so freely that her ringlets bobbed up and down below her bonnet. *"Touché,"* she said.

Any additional mutual evasions were prevented by the appearance of Sproul, the butler, bringing word of the arrival of the Harcourt chaise containing the twins and their mother.

Lord Ashley handed Gwen into the carriage, and her portmanteau and bandboxes were wrestled onto the roof. After an exchange of kisses and the fluttering of handkerchiefs, the driver snapped his whip, the four matched bays obediently surged forward, the carriage rounded the sweep of the drive, passed between the two towering trees that gave Twin Oaks its name, and was gone.

Lord Ashley turned to his younger daughter. "Shall we walk in the east garden?" he asked her.

She glanced at him in surprise since a short while before in the breakfast parlor he had complained about a recurrence of his gout. When he offered her his arm, she nodded, and they set off along a graveled pathway leading around the side of the imposing house.

"Papa," she said when she saw him limping, "you should really carry a walking stick. All the sporting gentlemen in London have them."

"Never used a stick in my life, don't intend to begin using one now." For a time they walked in silence as she wondered what purpose, if any, her father had in walking with her. When broaching

70

what he considered delicate subjects, she knew, he often used a stroll as a pretext for serious discussions. He was also a master of circumlocution.

"Mrs. Harcourt's very stiff-necked," she said. "She reminds me somewhat of Lady Jersey."

"Ah, yes, Sally, she does seem haughty to some. Did you ever pause to consider, Maud, how Lady Jersey might view the matter? She's without question a leading light of London society. She believes the aristocracy, the cream of that society, has risen to the top in England through innate superiority, and there's no question in her mind that England is the greatest, most powerful empire in the world. Aren't you entitled to be a trifle haughty when you occupy such an exalted position at the very pinnacle of such an immense pile?"

"Papa, I suspect you're teasing me and that you don't believe a word of what you said."

"I may not, Maud, but I suspect Lady Jersey does." He walked a few steps and then suddenly turned to her to ask, "Did you enjoy yourself at the Plimsalls' last night?"

"I love to dance."

"Your partners weren't merely the usual Surrey lads. I couldn't help but notice that both Lord Montrain and M. Lusignon led you out."

"I suspect everyone in the county is aware of that fact by now." She caught her breath. "Oh, dear," she said, brushing a bee off her frock.

"Pay close heed to that bee," her father advised her. "Watch how he buzzes around the peonies, leaves them to fly on to the forget-me-nots to collect their nectar or pollen or whatever and then to the row of hollyhocks, only to eventually abandon

71

the flowers altogether and disappear from view, never to return."

What was her father attempting to tell her? "Papa," she said, "I don't quite understand."

"Some of our more romantic poets," he said, "have compared the beauty of flowers to that of young ladies." Closing his eyes as though in remembrance, he quoted:

'O, my love is like a red, red rose,
That's newly sprung in June.
O, my love is like the melody,
That's sweetly played in tune.

"Burns wrote that. The Scot was one of your mother's favorite poets." Lord Ashley opened his eyes. "I fear I've lost the thread of my discourse," he admitted.

Maud thought she understood what he'd meant to convey. "You were telling me about the bee." Suppressing a smile, she added, "The bee might leave our Twin Oaks garden to fly far, far away, perhaps even crossing the Channel to some unknown foreign land."

"Ahhh, yes, my point precisely; you always were quick of wit, Maud. The bee's destination could be France, to put a name to this foreign land."

"Papa, in this instance you have no cause to be perturbed. Can a mere bud attract a bee? I think not, and it was M. Lusignon himself who informed me I resembled a bud rather than a bloom."

"That French scoundrel! How dare he make

72

such an odious comment to my daughter? His attentions to you are quite outside of enough. Especially while he's enjoying the hospitality of my house."

Surprised by the suddenness and depth of her father's anger, she quickly said, "He was merely being flirtatious, Papa, nothing more. Many gentlemen of the *ton,* or so I'm told, are even more forward than M. Lusignon."

"Not in my day they weren't. There's a dangerous laxness abroad in the land for which I blame nothing more than example of the Prince himself."

She squeezed his arm, affectionately resting her head for a moment against his shoulder. "I have no predilection for M. Lusignon," she told him. "In fact, I wouldn't shed a single tear if he never spoke to me again." Only after the words left her mouth did it occur to her that she hadn't mentioned Lord Montrain. But her father wasn't referring to him, was he?

Lord Ashley looked fondly at his younger daughter. Although he believed in being impartial with his children and although he loved Gweneth dearly, Maud had always been his secret favorite. To him she seemed so young, so lacking in experience in the ways of an uncaring and dangerous world, so susceptible to all the slings and arrows of life. How terrible to be so young and reckless. May God protect you, Maud, he murmured under his breath.

Maud shook her head, wondering if her father had always been so cautious, so circumspect. He perceived dangers lurking everywhere, down every twilit garden path, even in the most innocent of dances. Her heart ached for him. How terrible to be old and fearful.

During the next few days, she saw little of M. Lusignon, catching a few glimpses of his many comings and goings, nothing more. Despite what she'd told her father, she found the Frenchman's seeming indifference to her both annoying and disappointing.

An afternoon visit to the pool in the glen did nothing to dispel her malaise, what Gwen would have called her fit of the dismals. The day had been hot and sultry, gnats rose in swarms to hover around her head, and even the brook proved to be a traitor as it whispered to her of loneliness.

She missed Gwen's company keenly, but she kept as busy as she could by helping to groom and exercise Ne'er-Do-Well. On the day before their departure for Guildford, restless and feeling forsaken, she asked Tom Whittaker, the head groom, to saddle Juno for her.

At first she rode aimlessly in the Twin Oaks park, down country lanes and across grassy fields, but after a time she realized she was near the monastery ruins, so she urged the mare in that direction.

Climbing to just below the crest of a hill, she reined in. The monastery, built by the Cistercians — an order described by Lord Ashley as always reforming yet never reformed — on the highest elevation in this part of Surrey, had once been a landmark visible for miles around. Closed almost three hundred years before by order of Henry

VIII, the confiscated lands, by means of a series of intricate transactions, had eventually found their way into the hands of the newly wealthy Plimsalls some eighty years before.

Dismounting, she tethered Juno to a branch of a tree and walked to the ruins. The great stone slabs of the floor were carpeted with moss while ivy had grown over the crumbling walls and up the sides of a tower that ended in a jagged thrust of rock as though the remains of the building was angered by God's indifference.

Just beyond the ruined tower were two huge oaks thought to be descendents of trees used by priestesses performing ancient druid rites. Some in the nearby village of Ashton believed human sacrifices had once been conducted on this hill with men imprisoned in large wicker baskets and then burned alive.

When Maud sat on a fallen block of stone to look across the tops of the trees, her heart lurched. Below her, no more than a quarter of a mile distant, stood Blackstone House. She'd completely forgotten that Lord Montrain's home was visible from the ruins.

Or had she?

Rising, she walked to the top of a knoll for a better view of Montrain's realm. In one of the fields beyond Blackstone House, a Gothic structure as dark and foreboding as its name, two farmers hoed between rows of seedlings, but no matter how long and hard she looked, Lord Montrain was not to be seen.

Disappointed, she was starting to return to her horse when she noticed that the grass under her feet had been recently trampled. Glancing about her, she saw unmistakable evidence that a horse had spent some time beneath a nearby box tree.

And what was this on the grass beside a large flat rock? Kneeling, she gingerly prodded the stubs of three extremely thin cigars with her gloved finger. Leaving the stubs where they lay, she sat on the rock, looked down the hillside, and found she had an unobstructed view of both Blackstone House and its extensive grounds.

As she rode back to Twin Oaks on a lane beside a hedgerow bordering the Plimsall estate, she pondered what she had discovered at the monastery ruins. Undoubtedly someone, a man, had tarried there for a considerable time watching Lord Montrain's home. Who had the watcher been? And what was his purpose? Puzzled, she shook her head.

Leaving the hedges behind, she came to the first of a row of whitewashed cottages with roofs of brown thatch where she smiled and nodded to a woman spinning flax on a wheel in her yard. Behind the next cottage a boy pumped water into a bucket. When she rode past what appeared to be the last of the cottages, she saw one more, smaller and meaner than the rest, looking like an unimportant afterthought.

When she recognized it as Old Cob's cottage, she experienced a twinge of guilt. How long had it been since she'd last visited Old Cob? Six months? Eight? No, even more time had slipped by, probably almost a year. How remiss she'd been!

Not only did she like Old Cob, she was obligated to him. Years before, when the old man—

he'd always seemed old to her—had worked as one of Tom's helpers at the Twin Oaks stables, he'd taken the time to teach her not only to ride but to love horses almost as much as he did himself. Old Cob, whose mother was a gypsy, had always been a veritable nonesuch with animals.

As she neared his cottage, three men filed through the front door into the yard, their voices raised in anger. What an unusual assortment, she thought, recognizing all of them. There was stout, jowly Mr. Herbert Crispin, S.S., the bailiff; Mr. Everett Smollett, the Plimsall's estate agent, who was lean to the brink of emaciation; and Old Cob himself, stocky, swarthy, bent with age, his hair gray, his mustache long and curled.

On seeing Maud, Crispin and Smollett doffed their caps while Old Cob, who was bareheaded, attempted to avoid her gaze. The three men stood waiting, tense, their argument suspended for the few minutes it would take her to offer them a ladylike smile of acknowledgement and pass on out of earshot. Something, however, made her slow Juno. Perhaps it was the look of hopeless resignation on Old Cob's face, perhaps it was the imp of the perverse that often led her to do the opposite of what others expected.

Reining in her mare at the end of the path leading to the cottage, she looked down at the three men, nodding briefly to the bailiff and the agent before turning to Old Cob. "I've been terribly remiss," she told him, "in not visiting you before now."

Old Cob, his eyes still averted from hers, mumbled something incomprehensible. The path to his cottage and his garden, she noticed, were sadly overgrown with weeds.

"If your guests are leaving," she went on, "I'll stay and we can talk. I wanted to ask you about Ne'er-Do-Well. He races next week at Guildford."

"We're *all* of us leaving, Lady Maud." Smollett, the agent, gave great emphasis to the "all."

"I trust there's been no trouble," she said.

"Nothing you should concern yourself about, Lady Maud," Smollett told her.

She looked a question at Smollett, but the agent remained tight-lipped.

"Precisely what sort of trouble, Mr. Smollett?"

"A matter of Plimsall estate business," he said. "Pray give my regards to Lord Ashley," he added dismissively.

"I intend to remain here until I find out what the trouble is," she told them.

Herbert Crispin, S.S, shook his head impatiently. As a child, Maud had thought the S.S. had been an officially conferred title or a degree from a university. Only a few years ago her father had explained that the initials were attached to his name by Crispin himself and that they stood for Sinner Saved. "The man's a Methodist," Lord Ashley added as though that fact explained everything.

"The long and short of it, Lady Maud," Crispin said, "is that Old Cob here's long past due paying his rent and Mr. Plimsall's patience has run out. So the court's ordered me to escort this 'gentleman' from the Plimsall premises."

"I've offered to escort Old Cob to the Middleton almshouse, but he's refused to go," Smollett added

78

in an aggrieved tone. "More than eighty years old and he prefers to shun Christian charity. If he starves to death in the forest, 'tis no fault of mine nor of Mr. Crispin here."

"Is this true?" she asked Old Cob.

Still not looking at her, the old man said, "Old Cob's not about to be shut away in no poor-house."

Crispin looked up at her. "Could you perhaps persuade him, Lady Maud?" he asked. "He won't listen to us, and that's a fact."

Maud well knew just how stubborn Old Cob could be. "If he's made up his mind . . ." She shook her head.

"What the Lord was thinking when He in His wisdom created gypsies, I'll never know," Crispin said. "Why, if He Himself was to speak from a burning bush here in Surrey and order Old Cob to heed us, do you think that'd make a farthing's worth of difference? Not likely."

"How much does he owe?" she asked Smollett.

"The rent-roll shows him eight pounds in arrears and he'll owe another three for the remainder of the year, making a total of eleven in all."

She drew in a deep breath. "Lord Ashley will pay the eleven pounds," she said. "Mr. Plimsall will have his money, all of it."

"Begging your pardon," Smollett said, moving the toe of his boot back and forth in the dirt at his feet, "but I don't think Lord Ashley will pay one penny of Old Cob's debts, let alone eleven pounds."

She felt her face redden. "If I say my father will pay," she told him, "then he'll pay."

79

"No!" Old Cob raised his head to look her full in the face. "Old Cob will never take a farthing from the likes of him."

She slid from the saddle to the ground before any of the men could step forward to help her. Going to the gypsy, she took his hand in both of hers. "Take it not from my father but from me," she pleaded, "because I'm obligated to you for all you did for me years ago. You taught me to ride; you shared your love of horses with me." She saw he was wavering. "For me, Bendigo," she said, using his given name, the name she knew he preferred. "Please."

Old Cob hesitated for a long moment before giving a grudging nod.

Turning to Smollett, she said, "Tell Mr. Plimsall he'll have his money tomorrow."

Smollett gave her an unenthusiastic half-bow.

Mr. Crispin, S.S., stepped forward to help her remount, but Old Cob stopped him by putting his hand on the bailiff's arm. Crispin started to protest, then shrugged and stood aside as the old man grasped Maud around the waist and lifted her into the saddle.

Her father would honor her pledge, she assured herself as she rode away. He would, wouldn't he?

She waited until after their six o'clock dinner before seeking out her father, finding him in his favorite armchair in his gun room cleaning a flintlock. A glass of whiskey sat on the table beside him while his right foot rested on his gout stool.

Sitting perched on the edge of a straight-backed chair facing him, she said, "I visited Old Cob at his cottage today."

After putting the flintlock to one side, Lord Ashley picked up his whiskey glass and stared at the light from the oil lamp glimmering in the dark brown liquid.

"Mr. Smollett and Mr. Crispin were there to evict him. He owes Mr. Plimsall the sum of eleven pounds."

Lord Ashley raised his glass to his lips and drank, saying nothing.

"At the ball last week," she pushed on, "Georgie Plimsall told me his father had recently paid more than three times that amount for an enameled French snuffbox from the reign of Louis XIV."

"The price Mr. Plimsall pays for French snuffboxes hardly signifies."

"You can't mean to say a snuffbox is worth more than a man's life? Old Cob refused to go with them to the Middleton almshouse. He told them he'd rather starve to death in the forest."

"Old Cob's a free man able to choose for himself." Lord Ashley sat up straighter, wincing when his foot slid from the stool to the floor. "Don't try to work your feminine wiles on me, miss. I can clearly discern where this conversation is leading and my answer is an unequivocal no. I'm in no manner responsible for Old Cob, and under no circumstances will I be responsible for him."

She clutched her hands together in her lap and drew in a deep breath. "You may not be obligated to him, but I've made his welfare my responsibility," she said. "I'd like Old Cob to help me train Ne'er-Do-Well, if not for next week's race, then for next month's Newmarket Canterbury Stakes. So I promised to pay Mr. Plimsall his eleven pounds."

"You what?" Her father slammed his fist on the table. "Damme, you've allowed that old gypsy to cozen you. Do you expect me to become the benefactor of every impoverished worth-nothing in this county? If I did, before long you and I'd be the ones on the way to the almshouse."

Tears gathered in her eyes; she wanted to flee from her father's disapproving wrath. No, running away was childish and would accomplish nothing. "I gave them my word," she said. "The word of a Hawthorn."

"By God, you're as wrong-headed as—" He floundered for a name other than the one he had in mind. "As your mother," he finished lamely when he failed to think of one.

Maud stared at him in shocked silence. It was the first time she'd ever heard him say a word against her mother.

Lord Ashley shook his head as though he'd surprised himself. "You must realize she wasn't perfect, your mother." His voice was husky. "After all, no one is."

"Of course not." She knew no one was perfect, and yet she'd always thought of her mother as possessing all virtues and no faults. To realize she hadn't came as a revelation to Maud.

"Old Cob was a thief," her father said, "as are most if not all gypsies. I had to send him packing years ago."

"A thief? I can't believe—"

Her father silenced her with a wave of his hand. "Don't argue with me, Maud. He was a thief. Tom Whittaker caught him stealing. I wanted to spare you, so I never made you privy to this before. I see I was wrong; I should have." He sighed. "Since you pledged your word, Plimsall shall have his eleven pounds tomorrow. But Old Cob is not to set foot on Twin Oaks land. Do you lay hold of that, Maud?"

She went to her father, and when she knelt at his side, he put his hand on her head. "Yes, Papa," she said. "I don't know how to thank you."

She was so young, he thought, so disposed to act without considering all of the consequences. Would she ever come to see the world as it actually was, not as she hoped it might be?

He was so old and set in his ways, Maud thought. Would he always think of his purse before listening to his heart? Couldn't he understand that this world could be made so much better than it was?

Chapter Six

"Mrs. Wilcomb wishes to see you in her bed-chamber before you depart, Lady Maud," Sproul told her early on the morning they were to leave for Guildford.

Maud hurried up the stairs to Mrs. Wilcomb's room in the east wing. When she found her father's second cousin sitting in an easy chair wrapped in a shawl despite the warmth of the day, she felt a pang of dismay as she realized how much Mrs. Wilcomb had aged in the last few years.

"Turn around, my dear," Mrs. Wilcomb said, "and let me look at you."

As Maud pirouetted, she glimpsed herself in the mirror over the dressing table. Her high-waisted periwinkle blue gown and navy blue spencer were accented by her white neck scarf and a narrow-brimmed bonnet of the same color. She carried a furled white parasol decorated with clusters of blue polka dots.

"You look lovely," Mrs. Wilcomb said. "And to think you designed the gown yourself. I'm so disappointed I won't be able to witness the stares you'll attract from all the young men at Guild-ford."

"You're certain you can't come with us?"

"Unfortunately, my condition's worse today, so I'm afraid I'm not quite up to all the jouncing of the carriage ride followed by an inhospitable bed at the inn." Mrs. Wilcomb suffered from a recurring pain in her lower back.

"I'm sorry," Maud said. "I know how much you want to watch Ne'er-Do-Well run."

"If the truth be known, I think it was more that I wanted the pleasure of seeing you watch him run. For your sake, Maud, I'll be praying for a miracle. You love that horse more than he deserves."

"Ne'er-Do-Well won't need a miracle to win," Maud protested. "Tom says he has a sporting chance."

"I'm certain he has that." Doubt threaded through Mrs. Wilcomb's words. "But I didn't ask you to come all the way up here to discuss a horse race. The fact is, I was rummaging through one of my old trunks in the attic yesterday, admittedly a foolish thing to do considering my condition, when I came across a memento that I thought might interest you." She glanced at the pictures on the wall of her bedchamber. "First bring me the two silhouettes."

Maud lifted the small framed pictures of herself and Gwen from their hooks and placed them on Mrs. Wilcomb's lap. Lord Ashley had commissioned Noah Osman of Bond Street to fashion the portraits — created by using scissors to cut the thick black paper — as gifts from his daughters to Mrs. Wilcomb.

85

"And now look at what I discovered in my trunk." Mrs. Wilcomb lifted a larger framed silhouette from the floor beside her chair and held it in both hands above those of the Hawthorn sisters.

The picture from Mrs. Wilcomb's trunk was not only of a more ancient vintage, it had obviously been devised in a different manner. Maud suspected the silhouette of the head and bust had been outlined in pencil on white paper and then painted black.

"Mr. Jarman used a light to throw the shadow on the paper," Mrs. Wilcomb explained.

Maud frowned. Although the hair in the older silhouette was drawn back in a bun, the features were recognizably her own. "Isn't that odd," she said, "for if I didn't know better I'd believe I sat for this."

"Not as odd as all that, Maud. I'll admit it looks like you but, of course, it isn't. The old silhouette's of your mother when she was your age."

A shiver ran down Maud's spine as she stared in astonishment at the two pictures. "But I don't look at all like Mama," she protested. "Gwen does, but I don't. Everyone says so."

"Then perhaps everyone's thinking more of the portrait downstairs than of your mother herself. Admittedly Gwen has your mother's light coloring and the same shade of brown hair. Other than that, this silhouette speaks for itself." Mrs. Wilcomb smiled tenderly. "Some girls bloom early, others late. I showed you this, Maud, because I suspect you sometimes think of yourself as being plain. You're not plain, not at all. You're a lovely young woman growing lovelier with each passing day."

Maud, still looking from one silhouette to the other in wonderment, shook her head as the older woman's words made the color rise to her face. "What was she like?" she asked.

"Your mother? She was beautiful, spirited yet amiable, deeply religious, inclined to be stubborn. I suppose you know her family quietly opposed the match with your father, but your mother was bound and determined to marry him, and so of course she had her way."

"No, I didn't know."

"When he was young, your father had a reputation as a rake with his gaming and carousing. Witty, yes, and handsome, certainly, yet devil-may-care to a fault. Everyone predicted marriage wouldn't change him, but they were proved wrong. He became a devoted husband and father. I'm surprised, though, he's never remarried."

Her father marry again? The thought had never seriously occurred to Maud. Why, he was old!

"After all," Mrs. Wilcomb went on, "he was only forty-six last March."

Probably for someone in their eighties, Maud thought, forty-six seemed young. "I've never pictured Papa in quite that way," she said.

"He's always had a temper," Mrs. Wilcomb said, "and if you keep him waiting any longer you'll see evidence of it. So you'd best be on your way."

Maud kissed the older woman on the cheek. "Thank you for showing me the silhouettes and telling me about Mama," she said. She turned to leave but paused in the doorway when Mrs. Wilcomb called after her.

"Remember this, Maud," she said, "even the most beautiful garden the world has ever known had a serpent lurking in it."

"I'll remember."

She knew Mrs. Wilcomb referred to the Garden of Eden and the serpent that enticed Eve to eat the apple. Was she also thinking of the Plimsall garden where M. Lusignon had walked with her? She sighed in exasperation. Did everyone see her as so feather-witted she couldn't look after herself?

She rode to Guildford in the traveling chaise with her father as her only companion. Gwen was driving directly to Guildford from Epsom. M. Lusignon, visiting in London, expected to stop there to watch Ne'er-Do-Well race. As for Ne'er-Do-Well himself, Tom and another groom had taken him to Guildford the day before.

Now, idly watching the dust rise from the chaise's wheels to form a plume behind them, she congratulated herself. Most of the morning had already gone by, and she hadn't thought of Lord Montrain. Well, she admitted, perhaps he had crossed her mind once or twice, but she had immediately banished him.

She must concentrate on Tom Whittaker since something about the head groom had been tugging at her memory since her conversation with her father the evening before. Maud marshaled all she knew. Married, he'd been hired at a mop fair, coming to work at Twin Oaks before she, Maud, was born. His daughter had married an Ashton lad only last year while his son—

Of course! She vaguely remembered the son, a sullen youth also named Tom, helping his father and Old Cob in the stables when she was a child.

Then, or so she'd been told, the boy had suddenly run off from home to live with relatives in London.

"Papa," she asked, "whatever became of young Tom?"

Lord Ashley, who had been deep in communion with his own thoughts, blinked. "Young Tom?" he repeated.

"The son of Tom Whittaker."

Shaking his head dolefully, her father said, "A bad 'un, young Tom was. You'd get no quarrel from anyone about that. The lad was transported to New South Wales ten or more years ago. To the best of my knowledge he still makes his home down under."

"Transported for what reason?"

"Thievery of one sort or another. He was caught redhanded on Brook Street in Mayfair a short time after he ran off from Twin Oaks. I did my best for the lad—more for old Tom's sake than the boy's. Saved the cutpurse from the gallows, I expect."

Maud nodded to herself, almost certain she'd solved the mystery. The odds were the boy had been a thief before going to London—a leopard didn't change its spots—and Tom had shielded his son by blaming Old Cob, a convenient scapegoat since he was part gypsy. She wondered if this was the time to point out the likelihood of young Tom's guilt to her father.

"We're almost to Guildford," Lord Ashley said, a sense of expectancy in his voice.

Better to wait, Maud told herself. She'd talk to Old Cob first to learn the details of what had happened years before and then confront her father with the facts. Surely he'd listen and agree to give Old Cob permission to help train Ne'er-Do-Well.

They stayed overnight at the crowded Beckworth's Inn. The Guildford race meeting lasted a week and accommodations were booked well in advance.

The next forenoon, the day of Ne'er-Do-Well's race, her father hired a carriage to drive them to the racecourse. As soon as she stepped down to the ground, she felt the throbbing hubbub of a Guildford race day. Overhead small fleecy clouds scurried across the blue sky. The June breeze stirred the treetops and billowed the flags and bunting on the roof of the newly built grandstand.

Whips snapped and drivers shouted as carriages of every size and shape rumbled to and fro; she recognized hackney coaches down from London, four-in-hands, landaus, curricles, gigs, and perch phaetons. Spectators, many carrying telescopes or opera glasses, crowded the tops of carriages left without their horses beside the rope enclosing the racecourse.

"I can almost taste the excitement in the air," said Maud.

"It's the stir of hope in every breast," said her father. "Before the day's first race is run, any and all dreams are possible."

"My dream is that Ne'er-Do-Well will win."

"I expect him to go off at ten or more to one. Since Ne'er-Do-Well's ours, I feel obliged to back him with a guinea or two, but if he weren't, I confess I'd lay my money on Vulcan, Lord Montrain's horse. Even though it's against my principles to back the favorite."

Maud shook her head, disappointed. First Mrs. Wilcomb, now her father. Was she the only one with faith in Ne'er-Do-Well?

Since it lacked a quarter of an hour until the first race — Ne'er-Do-Well was entered in the Guildford Stakes, the fifth race of the day — Maud unfurled her parasol before taking her father's arm to stroll along the rope surrounding the grass course. She was pleased to see that today he walked without a limp.

"Racing's a great promoter of what the French call *fraternité*," her father said. "We'll see all kinds in Guildford today, from princes to paupers, from duchesses to drabs."

And, she suspected, wives and *chère-amies*, dowdies and young women she'd heard Gwen refer to as "dashing chippers who damped their muslins."

"And they're all dressed to the nines," she said. "What a rainbow of colors."

She admired lavender, gray, pale yellow, green, and rose gowns, white cotton frocks worn over frilled petticoats, pink and white stockings, gay bonnets and multihued parasols. As for the men, she saw dandies sporting narrow-waisted coats, tight trousers, white neckcloths and chicken-skin gloves mingling with countrymen wearing frock coats, buckskins, and top boots.

She overheard the ladies talking of clothes and food and parties; the men, of drink and horses and wagering.

As they started toward Ne'er-Do-Well's stable, she watched her father touch his hat to ladies of his acquaintance, noticed the coquettish smiles some of them gave him in return. Mrs. Wilcomb's words had forced her to consider him in a differ-

91

ent light, as a man as well as a father. She found her new perspective rather unsettling.

"Half the pickpockets in London are undoubtedly here today," her father said, "enjoying the opportunities presented by this horrible squeeze. I've recognized several notorious touts as well."

"And what are touts, Papa?"

"You might say they're a higher class of pickpocket since instead of utilizing the skill of their fingers, they depend on the persuasiveness of their tongues. One of the more formidable of their number, a thorough scoundrel known as Gentleman Jim, always claims to have information direct from the stable.

"His bit of gammon is to convince a gentleman with a heavy purse that the next race has been prearranged and he's been fortunate enough to be informed of the intended winner. If the horse by some happenstance should lose, Jim will ask for nothing. If he wins, Gentleman Jim collects his ten-percent commission. Or perhaps as much as fifteen."

"And does he actually know the winner before the race is run?"

"Of course not. He has no more idea than you or I, probably less. Gentleman Jim doesn't care who wins; he's playing a more devious game. If there are seven horses entered in the race, he'll convince seven different gentlemen to place their money on seven different horses. So he's bound to have given the winner's name to one grateful punter, and all without risking a single farthing of his own."

"How shameful."

"I fear most people would think him rather clever."

"There are too many dishonest men in the world as it is." Seeing Tom Whittaker lounging against the gate to Ne'er-Do-Well's stall, she added, "They seem to be everywhere you turn."

When he saw them, the head groom straightened, doffed his cap, and nodded respectfully.

"And how's Ne'er-Do-Well?" her father asked.

"Fit and ready to run," Tom said. "And I've hired that jockey from Tuscany you wanted, Louis Nannini. He's one of the best."

When Ne'er-Do-Well put his head over the gate, Maud stroked his neck and the horse nuzzled her. "And what instructions do you intend to give the jockey?" she asked Tom, trying to keep any hint of her newfound distrust of the groom from her voice.

"Just as we all agreed, Lady Maud. I told him to go to the front of the pack directly after the start and let them come to him if they can. I'd say Ne'er-Do-Well has a sporting chance to win the hogshead of claret if he can outlast Lord Montrain's Vulcan."

"Did I hear you mention Vulcan?" Gwen, looking vibrant in an almond and green gown worn with a shallow-crowned bonnet, waved goodbye to the Harcourt twins and joined them. "We've just come from seeing him," she said as they left the stall and made their way past the paddock to the grandstand.

How surprising, Maud thought, since Gwen had always professed to be afraid of horses. She seldom rode and had hurt Maud by ignoring Ne'er-Do-Well. On the other hand, considering who

93

owned Vulcan, perhaps it wasn't so surprising after all.

Gwen gave a mock shudder. "He's a magnificent brute, tall and dark and possessing an unmistakable air of arrogance."

Maud glanced sharply at her sister, wondering if she meant to describe the horse or his master or both. Holding her tongue proved an effort, but she conquered the impulse to ask. A moment later, hearing Gwen humming, she again glanced at her sister. Evidently Gwen had discovered two new interests, horses and music.

"What is that air you're humming?" Maud asked.

Gwen flushed vividly. "Was I humming?" she said. "I suppose I must have been. I couldn't help myself: it's such a lovely, lovely day."

Maud frowned as they walked on. Had something happened during Gwen's visit at the Harcourts'? Her sister certainly wasn't acting the least bit like herself.

After seating his daughters in his owner's box, Lord Ashley excused himself to "engage in some transactions of a monetary nature," presumably at the ring where the bookmakers gathered to chalk the odds on their boards.

After nodding to the Athertons in their nearby box, Gwen leaned toward Maud to whisper in her ear. "I must admit to feeling positively giddy today," she said. "I find myself sighing for no reason at all and smiling at absolutely nothing. Isn't it wonderful just to be alive?"

"Are you feverish? Perhaps you're coming down with *la grippe*."

"Oh, I don't think so, dear sister . . ." Gwen

94

suddenly drew in her breath.

Maud, following the direction of Gwen's gaze, saw Lord Montrain standing a short distance away. He swept off his top hat and gave them a gallant bow.

Gwen gripped Maud's wrist. "Please, Maud," she pleaded in a low voice, "if Papa asks, tell him I'm with the Harcourt twins. You will, won't you?"

Maud hesitated, then nodded.

Rising, Gwen started walking rapidly toward Lord Montrain only to stop and return. Once more she lowered her voice. "You entertain no particular feelings of fondness for John—" Catching herself, she went on, "—for Lord Montrain, do you, Maud?"

"I hardly know him," Maud said through tight lips.

Gwen nodded and hurried away.

When Lord Ashley returned to the box shortly thereafter, he frowned as he looked about him. "Where's your sister?"

"I saw her with the Harcourt twins." Which wasn't quite a falsehood, Maud assured herself, since she had seen her with the twins earlier. She sighed. Now she'd told two half truths within the space of five minutes. The older you were, the more complicated life became.

Maud and her father watched the first four races from their box before walking to the paddock for the saddling of Ne'er-Do-Well and the other horses competing in the Guildford Stakes. When they returned to their box, Maud found Rob Atherton waiting for her.

"Charles Headley's saving a spot along the rope near the finish line," he told Lord Ashley. "May

Maud watch the race with us from there?"

"If she wishes," Lord Ashley told him.

"You cheer for Ne'er-Do-Well from here," Maud told her father, "and I'll shout encouragement from down below." Linking arms as two comrades might, she and Rob set off to join Charles Headley.

After parading past the grandstand, the horses were walked around a turn in the track and disappeared behind a cluster of trees. At Guildford, where the track was shaped like an ironing board, the spectators in and near the grandstand were able to watch the progress of the race only from the time the horses reached the vicinity of the half-mile post to the finish post.

A track steward in a tower near the starting line raised his flag. The crowd hushed. The flag swooped down. All around Maud the cry went up: "The horses have started!"

Maud watched the spot where the thoroughbreds would appear with a mixture of hope and trepidation. The seconds dragged by. Half a minute. More. In front of the rope a rider on a gray gelding trotted back and forth snapping a whip to keep the more rowdy spectators from venturing onto the racecourse.

"There they are," Rob shouted, pointing.

Maud leaped up and down. "Ne'er-Do-Well's in the lead!" she cried.

"By five or more lengths!" Rob spun her around and hugged her as he had so many times when they were young.

All at once he reddened, released her, and drew back. "I'm devilishly sorry," he said, "I quite forgot myself. I keep thinking of you the way you

96

were."

Maud stared at him in surprise and then she, too, blushed and stepped awkwardly away. "There's no need to apologize," she told him. How peculiar, she thought. Rob and Charles and so many of the others seem to have remained young while I've grown older.

Maud looked past him at the horses. Her heart sank, for Ne'er-Do-Well's lead was now only three lengths. A huge black horse gained on him. Vulcan!

"Hold on, Ne'er-Do-Well!" she urged.

One by one the horses momentarily disappeared from her view as the track dropped into what was popularly known as the "Guildford Dip." When Ne'er-Do-Well reappeared, his lead had shrunk to a mere length. Vulcan ran second with two other horses racing in the middle of the track just behind him. Maud pounded her gloved fist into her palm, willing Ne'er-Do-Well to persevere.

The horses rounded the turn and entered the straightaway in front of the grandstand. The crowd was standing, shouting, urging, pleading.

"I can't tell who's leading." Maud had to raise her voice to be heard.

"Still Ne'er-Do-Well," Rob shouted back. "Wait." He groaned. "Vulcan's gaining!"

Vulcan swept past Ne'er-Do-Well. She heard cries of "Vulcan! Vulcan!" from all sides. The horses thundered toward her. Two more passed the fading Ne'er-Do-Well. Vulcan pounded by in front of her and passed the finish post far in front. Two, no, three other horses followed before the sweat-stained, tired Ne'er-Do-Well crossed the line.

As tears gathered in Maud's eyes, she averted

her head so Rob and Charles wouldn't be witness to her anguish. She'd been so confident, so full of hope, and now those hopes had been dashed.

"They're leading Vulcan into the winner's enclosure," Charles told her. "Don't you want to watch?"

Shaking her head, Maud dabbed at her eyes. While she wasn't a poor loser, she told herself, she certainly didn't want to see the glow of victory on Lord Montrain's face when he received his purse money and the winner's hogshead of claret. After all, he hadn't won the race, Vulcan had.

"Now all of them are congratulating Montrain," Rob reported. "By Jove, he cuts quite the dashing figure." Rob turned to her. "Don't be disheartened, Maud," he said consolingly. "Ne'er-Do-Well will have other chances. There's the Canterbury Stakes at Newmarket next month if your father chooses to run him there."

She looked up at Rob, trying to force herself to smile since he was right. Of course there would be other races. Hadn't she, though, lost more than a race today? She and Rob could never again share the camaraderie they had once known. Somehow, without even noticing, she'd left her childhood behind, and that loss lasted forever.

Maud sighed, and now she did smile, sadly. "You're right," she told him, taking his arm and starting to walk with him back to the Ashley box. From the corner of her eye she caught sight of Lord Montrain at the center of a circle of admirers. Seeing Maud, he excused himself away and hurried across the grass to her.

"Let me talk to him alone," she told Rob. Reluctantly, he retreated.

Lord Montrain gallantly raised his hat. "You look quite fetching this afternoon, Lady Maud," he said.

Now that she was facing him, the feelings that had been dammed within her for so long, her disappointment over the outcome of the race, her anger at what she saw as his betrayal, her sense of loss, all burst loose in a great torrent of words.

She knew she had to speak quickly before his presence discomfited and disarmed her. When they were apart words sprang easily to her lips, when together she more often than not found herself tongue-tied.

"At the Plimsalls' ball," she told him, keeping her voice low so no one else would hear, "you slipped away with my sister and then returned to throw me a sop by waltzing with me, and now today you've done the same thing exactly. Do you know who you remind me of, Lord Montrain? You're a second Gentleman Jim, except you practice your wiles with women instead of horse races. You find seven young ladies and bestow your elaborate and deceitful compliments on each of them with the hope that you'll win the heart of at least one. Such a stratagem is not about to succeed with Lady Maud Hawthorn, and if you believe it is, you're quite mistaken."

She paused to catch her breath.

His eyebrows rose. "Gentleman Jim?" he asked. "To the best of my knowledge, I'm not acquainted with the chap. As for the seven young ladies, I fear I don't understand, Lady Maud."

"You may not understand what I mean, but I understand full well what your intentions are." She realized her voice had risen, causing people to stare, but she couldn't help herself. "And as for your hogshead of claret, Lord Montrain, I sincerely hope you proceed to choke on it."

He bowed. "Perhaps we might continue this conversation at a more convenient time," he said. "Good afternoon, Lady Maud." He turned abruptly and strode off, disappearing into the crowd.

So he had naught to say to defend himself, Maud thought. Good. He as much as acknowledged he's in the wrong.

At the same time she was congratulating herself on routing him, she heard a faint whisper from her more prudent self warning her that she'd gone too far.

She drew in a deep breath and let it out slowly. What was done was done.

About to make her way to her father's box, she noticed M. Lusignon, dressed in black as he had been on his arrival at Twin Oaks, standing some distance away. The faint smile curling his lips told her he'd observed her brief encounter with Lord Montrain.

As she watched him, M. Lusignon removed a long thin cigar from his pocket, clipped off one end, lit the cigar, and began to smoke.

Chapter Seven

Of course, Maud reminded herself in the days that followed, M. Lusignon wasn't the only man who smoked long thin cigars. She didn't, though, know of any others at Twin Oaks, or in the county of Surrey for that matter, and so she strongly suspected the Frenchman had been the one watching Lord Montrain's Blackstone House from the monastery ruins.

It was possible that M. Lusignon had no ulterior motive but merely enjoyed observing others out of idle curiosity or in an attempt to discover their secrets. He certainly watched her. Several times since returning from the Guildford races she had glanced across the room and found his appraising gaze fixed on her. Each time he had looked quickly away.

He didn't, however, make any attempt to engage her in conversation beyond polite remarks regarding English weather as compared to French (he preferred the climate of his homeland) or Ne'er-Do-Well's condition (he sincerely hoped the race hadn't effected the horse's fitness) or the hospitality of the Hawthorns during his stay at Twin Oaks (he found it exceptionally gracious). Despite his innocuous words, M. Lusignon's continued presence in the house made her uncomfortable. Exactly why, she couldn't explain, perhaps merely because she sensed he understood her much better than she understood him.

When she happened to breathe in the aroma from his thin cigars, however, she was less apt to be reminded of M. Lusignon than of the bitter scent of the smoke from the bridges she'd so heedlessly burned at Guildford. Even though, she admitted ruefully, any bridges between herself and Lord Montrain had been of the most flimsy and temporary variety and therefore easily destroyed.

As soon as Tom assured her that there was no doubt Ne'er-Do-Well had emerged from the Guildford Stakes in "top of the trees" condition, she went looking for her father, finding him ensconced in the smoking room.

"The Canterbury Stakes at Newmarket?" he repeated in answer to her question. "You want me to run Ne'er-Do-Well at Newmarket next month?"

"He can do better than he did at Guildford. I know he can. And Tom thinks so, too."

" 'The horse has a sporting chance.' I can almost hear Tom say the words. Tell me, Maud, exactly where did Ne'er-Do-Well finish at Guildford?

"Fifth in a field of nine," she had to admit.

"He could do much better than that at Newmarket and still fail to place." Lord Ashley raised his hands, palms up. "It's not that I wouldn't like to enter a horse in the Canterbury Stakes, but we must face facts. Up north he'd be up against competition even stronger than at Guildford. Not only will Vulcan be entered, there will be horses from

Epsom and even the filly Ailema may race. She's undefeated in five starts."

"What an odd name. Ailema sounds like a tropical disease."

"Lord Ealing's only daughter is named Amelia. Ailema is Amelia spelled backwards."

Maud couldn't repress a smile. "Dumb," she said.

"I beg your pardon?"

"I was wondering what Ne'er-Do-Well would be called if you'd chosen to name him after me. Maud spelled in reverse is D-a-u-m."

"Quite so." He shrugged off her comment. "If you're attempting to distract me from the matter at hand, miss, I promise you won't succeed." Her father leaned forward and put his hand lightly on Maud's shoulder. "You must learn to be realistic," he told her. "Entering Ne'er-Do-Well in the Canterbury Stakes is an expensive undertaking, and the state of my purse these days is anything but healthy."

Her eyes opened wide in surprise.

"Don't be overly perturbed," he told her. "I'm not predicting that the bailiffs will soon descend on Twin Oaks and proceed to incarcerate me at Marsalsea, nor am I about to flee across the Channel to Antwerp. I may, however, be forced to sell some of our land."

Maud gasped in dismay. "The Hawthorn land? I hadn't realized we were so much in debt, Papa." She went to him and hugged him, then kissed him on the cheek. "On my honor, I'll not say another word to you about Newmarket," she promised as she started to leave the room.

"If there's anything else you want, Maud . . ."

"There's nothing, Papa, nothing at all."

She remembered Lord Montrain striding away from her at Guildford. At least nothing her father had the power to grant her, she told herself with a wan smile.

Even though her dream of Ne'er-Do-Well racing and winning at Newmarket had been dashed, Maud was still determined to do her best to clear Old Cob's name. Therefore, on a hot and sultry afternoon on one of the last days of spring, she donned her favorite riding habit — a dress of white lawn with a velvet belt, a spencer of forest green, and gloves and jockey cap of the same color — and asked Tom to saddle Juno.

If only Gwen had enjoyed riding, she would have asked her sister to accompany her even though Gwen had been living in a world of her own ever since the day of the Guildford races. Gwen either spent her time reading novels of gothic romance, sitting on the terrace with her eyes closed and from time to time sighing, or wandering about the house with a distracted look on her face.

Maud decided to ride to Old Cob's cottage along the same route she'd followed the month before. After dismounting at the monastery ruins, she walked around the top of the hill, searching for evidence of further visits by the cigar smoker. She found none.

Sitting on the same flat boulder, shaded by a giant oak, she gazed down at Blackstone House. She saw a horseman riding along a road flanked by trees between the gatehouse and her vantage point, but he disappeared from her view beneath the brow of the hill before she could identify him. Otherwise there was no activity visible at Lord Montrain's.

What, she asked herself, had become of his American friend, Philip Faurot? Following his brief appearance at the Plimsalls' ball, she hadn't seen him again. Was he ill? Had he sailed from England to return to his home in New Orleans? He seemed an elusive shadow, a will-o'-the-wisp, rather than a flesh and blood person.

She shouldn't, she admonished herself, spend her time fretting about people who were no concern of hers, people such as Philip Faurot and Lord Montrain. Instead she should be looking forward with eager anticipation to next winter and her coming-out Season. She frowned, wondering if there might be some flaw in her character since, while Gwen had thoroughly enjoyed her moment in the London sun, Maud, unaccountably, felt otherwise. She would, if the truth be known, be more than a little relieved once the next year was over and done with.

Closing her eyes, she imagined that many years had passed, that her Season, a great success, was far behind her. She saw herself in an elegant open carriage, its interior lined with blue velvet, riding in Hyde Park at the fashionable hour of five accompanied by a very handsome, rather haughty-appearing older woman."

"My dear Maud," said Lady Jersey, for indeed she was the handsome older woman, "I must solicit your opinion regarding a matter of the utmost delicacy."

"Does this by any chance concern a certain Miss Imogene Guernsey?"

"How perspicacious you are, Maud!" Lady Jersey exclaimed. "Yes, it most definitely does involve Miss Guernsey. The problem, though frightfully important, is simply stated: Should she or should she not be placed on Almack's List to receive a voucher for our next Season?"

Maud, even though she had been expecting the question ever since Miss Guernsey had tearfully appealed to her to intercede in her behalf, paused several minutes before replying. "Her credentials are seemingly impeccable," she said, "family, position, means, modesty, wit, amiability, charm, beauty. She possesses them all in abundance."

"Admittedly. And yet —" Lady Jersey sighed as she shook her head sadly. "I'm certain you've heard of her lamentable transgression. The scandal's been spread by every prattlebox in town."

"I'm aware she had the temerity, nay, the audacity, call it what you will, to dance the waltz in London before her coming-out Season. What in the name of heaven could she have been thinking?"

Lady Jersey placed her gloved hand on Maud's arm. " 'Twas but a youthful impulse, or so she maintains, a devastating combination of a single glass of champagne, the presence of a dashing rake, a thoughtless moment.

"In and of itself," Lady Jersey went on, "one of our young ladies dancing a waltz at an inappropriate time means naught. We have, however, over the years established a code of conduct for our young ladies, and if we don't uphold it, if we waver in the slightest, all of Society is at risk. We must remember that the pagan barbarians are always massed outside our walls, ever ready to storm our gates, lusting to commit wanton acts of pillage, slaughter, and rapine. If once they gain entrance, we and all we hold dear will be swept into oblivion."

"Have no fear," Maud assured her. "The gravity of the situation isn't lost on me." She pursed her lips in thought "Did you know," she asked, "that I, too, was once guilty of dancing the waltz before my Season? Not in London, of course," she added hastily. "It was at a rather nondescript ball in Surrey."

Lady Jersey nodded. "I recall being apprised of that fact. I even believe I remember the name of your partner. Wasn't it Lord Montrain? Just prior to his disastrous concatenation of misfortunes?"

Recalling that time, Maud nodded wistfully. How young she'd been! How terribly foolish! And yet even now, so many years later, she couldn't think of Lord Montrain without a pang of regret for what might have been.

"As for Miss Guernsey," Maud said, putting all thoughts of Lord Montrain aside, "in due consideration of her many exemplary qualities, why don't we suggest to her, through a trusted intermediary of course, that she publicly apologize to you, Lady Jersey, for her single misstep and throw herself on your mercy. In that way, if you grant her an exception and give her a voucher, the code of Society is upheld while at the same time the patronesses of Almack's will be applauded for demonstrating their forgiving natures."

107

Lady Jersey pursed her lips, then nodded. "An excellent proposal. Though I must discuss your suggestion with Lady Castlereagh, the Princess, and the others, I'm confident they'll all be delighted to concur." Lady Jersey patted Maud's hand gratefully. "I knew I could rely on you, Maud. As always."

Maud smiled, savoring anew her status as Lady Jersey's most valued confidante. An instant later her smile faded when she espied a solitary wretch seated — no, more precisely, sprawled — beside the roadway. The beggar, for such he undoubtedly was, had sought the shade of a pedestal supporting a huge ornamental urn from which spewed a veritable fountain of greenery.

Speak of the devil, Maud murmured to herself, and he appears.

"Louis," she called to her coachman, the former jockey, Louis Nannini, "stop at once!" The carriage shuddered to a halt.

"That man lying beneath the urn," she told Louis, "bring him here so I may speak to him. Offer him a few pennies recompense if you must."

"Have your wits deserted you, Maud?" Lady Jersey asked. "Never have I seen a more ramshackle person in the Park. His kind aren't tolerated here. It is the law of the land — even though the law is unwritten. Surely he knows that. Why on earth do you wish to speak to him?"

"I believe this wretch, for surely he's that," Maud replied calmly, "is someone I knew years and years ago." "Notice his clothes, the dirty, faded blue coat, the soiled black trousers, the torn striped stockings, all once represented the height of fashion. See how he looks up at Louis with a certain haughty disdain imperfectly masked by his obsequiousness."

After Louis spoke to him, the derelict pushed himself to his feet, blinking in the sunlight and tottering unsteadily but refusing Louis's proffered assistance. As he approached the carriage he lurched from side to side.

Lady Jersey lowered her voice. "The wastrel," she said, "for I have no doubt he is one, gives every evidence of paying the price for a lifetime spent in debauchery and dissipation."

The bewhiskered derelict grasped the top of the wheel of their carriage to steady himself. After squinting his bleary eyes to look up at Maud and Lady Jersey, he removed his cloth cap to reveal thinning gray hair. "Your ladyships," he said in the husky voice of a five-bottle man, "I was not always as you see me now."

"I'm well aware of that, Lord Montrain," Maud said. "You are Lord Montrain, are you not?"

Lord Montrain—for indeed it was the former proud occupant of Blackstone House and no other—glanced apprehensively to his right and then to his left. "Your ladyship," he implored, addressing Maud, "pray have pity on this poor unfortunate by not revealing his true identity. My enemies, and I have many clever and unforgiving enemies, lurk everywhere. Those who instigated my incarceration at Marsalsea and those who forced me to bid adieu to my native land and flee to Antwerp still hound my every step even after these many years."

"Your secret is safe with us," Maud assured him.

How could she help remembering that when she was young, it seemed ages ago, she'd loved Lord Montrain? He'd been her love when her heart was tender and thus an easy prey for Cupid's arrows. Nonetheless, the man who was a woman's first love was always special. No matter whether he deserted her, betrayed her, eventually came to bore her, still he occupied a niche in her heart containing, perhaps, his faded likeness and a bouquet of withered flowers.

She sighed since now all she felt for him was pity. "You don't recognize me, do you?" she asked.

"I admit you have the advantage."

"You once knew me as Lady Maud Hawthorn."

Lord Montrain's mouth gaped in astonishment. "You!" he exclaimed. "Today you're acclaimed as the epitome of beauty, the most fashionable and wittiest woman in all of England. Word of your more than generous benefactions has spread far beyond these sceptered shores. And yet I remember you only as a slip of a girl."

"In your eyes that was all I was."

She turned to Louis, who through all of this exchange had stood to one side evidencing a studied disinterest. "Here, Louis, pray give these to Lord Montrain." She removed two sovereigns from her reticule.

"My dear Maud," Lady Jersey protested in an overloud voice, "I fear you're allowing your heart to rule your head. No matter who or what he once was, this poor unfortunate wretch is today

110

one of the dregs of society. No matter what he may promise you, he'll take your money and use it to further indulge his low appetites."

"Let him do with the money what he will," Maud said softly. "I owe him at least this much."

When Louis handed him the coins, Lord Montrain used his fingers to test his coat pocket for holes before slipping them inside. "God bless you," he said to Maud. Turning a withering look on Lady Jersey, he said, "If you believe I'll use this largess to hasten my descent into dissipation, madam, you're quite mistaken."

Lady Jersey expressed her disbelief in his promise with what could only be described as an unladylike snort.

"I believe you," Maud said, tears misting her eyes.

"I intend," Lord Montrain told her, "to at least partially redeem myself by disseminating the history of my downfall as a cautionary tale. I plan to use your generous gift to finance the publication of a pamphlet detailing the circumstances that led me to my present unfortunate state so others will be warned and not wander unwittingly from the path of temperance into the slough of temptation."

"Such a selfless undertaking could accomplish a world of good."

"Would you believe it was a hogshead of claret won in a horse race that started me on the downward slope? I've not only been overindulgent, I've been blind."

Maud gasped. "You're blind?" she asked. "I had no way of knowing."

" 'Tis not what you think. Not a blindness affecting the eyes, 'tis a blindness of my very heart and soul. I dare speak no more since you will think I wish to appeal to your sympathies, to your overabundant kindness. Let me only say my salvation was always near at hand and I failed to recognize it—nay, not it, her—for what she was." Lord Montrain stepped back and bowed in farewell.

A tear trickled down Maud's cheek. "Drive on, Louis," she ordered, her voice hoarse with the unique heartbreak reserved for what might have been.

As Louis mounted to the driver's perch, Lord Montrain dropped to his knees in the dirt at the side of the roadway.

The carriage started forward.

Lord Montrain steepled his hands in front of him. "God bless you, Lady Maud," he called after her.

Maud bit her lip to stifle a sob. She would not look back, she promised herself, she must not look back. She kept her vow until they had traveled at least a quarter of a mile when, no longer able to resist temptation, she turned and glanced behind the carriage. Her last sight of Lord Montrain, his pitiful image blurred by her tears, was of this once-proud man kneeling at the roadside with his steepled hands raised above his head . . .

Chapter Eight

Maud opened her eyes and blinked in the bright sunlight before adjusting the brim of her jockey cap to better shade her face. Rising, she brushed off the skirt of her riding habit.

When she looked below her at Blackstone House, she saw a gardener, a boy trotting at his side, trundling a wheelbarrow along a path. She saw a sway-backed horse slowly pulling a cart toward the fields, and, in the distance, sheep grazing on a grassy hillside.

She drew in a long breath and let it out in a sigh, for her daydream had left her with a clear yet undefined sense of loss. As though something valuable, something that would never come her way again, had been within her grasp and she had unwittingly allowed it to escape. Without ever knowing what it was.

Don't be a goose! she admonished herself. Her daydreams were nothing more than foolish imaginings; she wasn't about to allow them or anything, or anyone, to send her into a fit of the dismals. Glancing once more toward Lord Montrain's Blackstone House, she raised her chin defiantly.

Suddenly a tingling ran up along her spine, and her skin prickled.

Someone was watching her, she had no doubt of it. Could it be M. Lusignon? She held, all her senses alert, but she saw and heard nothing out of the ordinary. No wind whispered overhead in the oaks; the hot sun had apparently silenced even the birds. Turning slowly, fully expecting her alarm to have been for naught, Maud gasped when she saw the figure of a man silhouetted against the blue of the sky.

Lord Montrain, gripping his riding whip with both hands, stood some twenty feet away with his gaze fixed on her. She was startled to see he wore a blue coat just as he had in her daydream, but his trousers were navy blue rather than black. Beside him the ruined tower of the monastery thrust darkly skyward.

He was hatless, and the sunlight glinted from his eyes. Though he remained motionless, she sensed a pulsing energy coiled within him, at present held precariously in check but threatening to burst violently forth at any moment.

Her heart pounded alarmingly. Only because he'd startled her, she told herself, for no other reason. After all, Lord Montrain wasn't here because of her. Undoubtedly he'd been at Blackstone House, had seen a stranger on the hill, and had ridden to investigate. He must, she realized, have been the horseman she'd observed a short time before.

"Maud!" he called.

She drew in her breath at his intimate address.

She felt as though he were reaching out to her, trying to draw her to him. She shivered, wanting to answer him, yet fearful her voice would reveal her turmoil, her longing to go to him, to have him share his innermost thoughts with her, and, she couldn't deny it, to have him touch her.

"Maud," he said again, his voice softer yet no less fervent, "come to me."

Without thinking, as though impelled by an inner need over which she had no control, she stepped toward him only to stop at once, shaking her head. No matter how much she longed to do his bidding, she knew she mustn't, for if she did, all reason would be overthrown and for her there would be no turning back. Ever.

He slapped his riding whip against his gleaming black boots, slapped it once, twice, three times, then hurled the whip impatiently to one side. He held out his hand to her. "Come to me, Maud," he commanded, his voice husky and intense.

For a breathless moment she wavered, poised between fear and desire, then she whirled away from him and ran. She ran across the moss-covered stones of the monastery floor, ran along the path from the crest of the hill to the cluster of trees where she'd tethered Juno, the horse whinnying as she neared her. Hurriedly leading the mare to one of the fallen granite stones, she used it as a mounting block, stepping to its top and pulling herself up into the sidesaddle.

Glancing behind her, she could no longer see Lord Montrain. Relief washed over her while at the same time she felt a strong undertow of disappointment. A regret such as Lord Wellington might have experienced after preparing elaborate fortifications only to have Napoleon's army fail to attack.

Urging Juno into a lope, she followed the track leading back to Twin Oaks, to home, to her father, to the safety of the familiar, to a haven far from this hilltop where druid priestesses once performed their pagan rites.

Following the path into a woods, she found herself in a veritable tunnel burrowed through the enclosing trees. Branches thick with leaves met and intertwined to form a canopy above her head and, by denying entry to the sun, created a world of perpetual twilight below.

Juno's hooves thudded on the dirt, lush foliage rushed by her in a blur, birds shrilled their cries of alarm. A doe, startled, raised its head at her approach then bounded from the path to disappear among the trees.

Hoofbeats thudded behind her. Glancing over her shoulder, Maud saw Lord Montrain astride a galloping black stallion. She gasped. It was Vulcan. How could she and Juno possibly outrun him?

Grasping her whip, she struck Juno's flank and felt the horse respond with a forward surge. Horse and rider burst from the grove at full gallop, leaving the shadows for the sudden blinding glare of sunlight, racing across a field white with daisies.

She heard Vulcan pound ever closer. The warm air tugged at her cap and hair, molding her skirts

116

to her legs. Her breath quickened. She heard a sound and looked to her right; he was there, beside her. He reached for Juno's reins, grasped them in one hand, and pulled back. Stifling a scream, she struck at him with her riding whip but, ignoring her, he reined in Vulcan, slowing and stopping Juno at the same time.

Maud, holding to the pommel, slid from her saddle to the ground. She ran from the path into the high grass through the daisies, her pulses quickening when she heard him running behind her, his footsteps coming closer and closer. Looking over her shoulder, she saw he was almost upon her, his eyes glinting, his hair tousled. She tripped, reached out to catch herself only to tumble face down on the grass amidst the daisies.

She twisted around onto her back and looked up to see him standing over her with his hands on his hips, his chest rapidly rising and falling, his face expressionless. He was no longer Lord Montrain. He was the Black Knight of her childhood dreams come to rescue her from the tower; he was her knight errant ready to defend her honor on the field of battle; he was a highwayman about to carry her off to his forest fastness. He was all of these, yet he was more since he was real.

Suddenly he dropped to his knees at her side.

"Why did you run from me, Maud?" he asked softly. "You know I'd never harm you. You do know that, don't you?"

She stared up at him. Yes, he was right, she did know without understanding how she knew.

117

Intuitively. She nodded slowly, shyly, all the while wondering if he could hear the pounding of her heart.

He reached to her, and she thought he was going to caress her face, but instead his fingers felt along the strap beneath her chin until he found the button. He twisted the button, the strap came loose, and with infinite care he removed her jockey cap, allowing her brown hair to spring free and halo her face.

"You're so beautiful," he murmured as he stared down at her, slowly shaking his head as though he couldn't believe the evidence of his eyes. "You're my beautiful druid priestess."

Held in thrall, unable to speak, she was conscious of him and him alone, his black wavy hair, his dark brown eyes, the pleasing curve of his lips. The violence she'd sensed in him before was gone, replaced by an infinite tenderness. When he leaned to her, she knew he meant to kiss her. She held her breath.

His lips barely touched hers, glided over hers in the lightest, most delicate, most delightful of caresses. She closed her eyes.

The massive wooden bar on the gate splintered, then broke with an explosive crack.

Maud reached up, wrapped her arms around his neck, and drew him down to her, kissing him for what seemed a breathless eternity. Realizing too late what she'd done, she gasped and turned her head to one side, opening her eyes but afraid to look at him for fear her will to resist would vanish like dew in the

118

warmth of morning sunlight.

He gripped her shoulders, lifting her. "Believe in me, Maud," he said.

For a moment she thought he meant to enfold her in his arms, to shower kisses on her cheeks, her eyelids, her parted lips, but he did not. Instead, his grip loosened, and he lowered her gently to the grass. His fingers caressed the ringlets on her forehead, and when she opened her eyes, she saw him reach to one side to pick daisies and then thread them into her hair to form a tiara of white flowers.

"If only I could give you diamonds," he told her. "You deserve a diadem of the finest jewels."

"I'd rather have the daisies," she said. It was true. How could any gems replace the flowers he'd picked for her?

"I believe you actually mean that." He smiled. "Any other young lady would prefer to have the diamonds. And that's one of the reasons you deserve them."

She tried to gather her wits, difficult as it was with him so near to her. "I'm not at all certain you're making any sort of sense," she said.

All at once he looked away from her as a pall seemed to envelop him. "Nothing in this world makes sense." He shook his head, his lips tightening in what appeared to her to be pain. "Whatever happens," he said, "I want you to believe in me. Do you promise you will?"

Confused, not understanding his meaning, nonetheless she nodded.

He kissed her quickly, then stood and, reaching

119

down with both hands, pulled Maud to her feet. When he started to lead her back to their horses, she leaned down and retrieved her cap, carrying it by the strap.

He lifted her into the saddle, his strength surprising and exciting her, but instead of mounting Vulcan, he tied his horse to Juno's saddle and, taking Juno's reins, led both horses along the path toward Twin Oaks.

She didn't understand why he chose not to ride beside her, why he walked like a pilgrim performing penance, but she said nothing. Instinctively she realized he wouldn't kiss her again. To Maud this moment was like the finest of crystal, lovely yet ever so fragile.

As soon as they saw the gray stone walls of Twin Oaks, he walked to her and when he gave her Juno's reins, he held and kissed her hand. She wondered if he intended to seek her pardon for his rashness. She wished he would since only if he did would she have the pleasure of forgiving him. But without a word he mounted Vulcan, wheeled the black horse, and rode off. Bemused, she watched him until he was out of sight before riding to the stable.

Still carrying her cap, she went into the house, leaving the daisies twined in her hair in the hope someone would see her and wonder at her floral adornment. To her chagrin she met only Sproul, and he, true to his calling, showed no reaction to the daisies, either by word or gesture.

In the library she pulled down the fourth volume of Gibbon's *The Decline and Fall of the Ro-*

man Empire, opened it at random and carefully inserted the daisies between the pages before returning the book to the shelf. The flowers, unlike the day, would last forever. Misty-eyed, she found herself smiling at nothing at all.

Much later Maud stood in front of the window of her bedchamber while the setting sun on this, one of the longest days of the year, tinted the clouds with delicate brushstrokes of rose and pink. An evening breeze sprang up, whispering high above her in the branches of the oaks, billowing the white curtains in her room—Maud didn't share the almost universal fear of drafts and fresh air—heralding a change in the weather.

She, too, had changed. She now knew that in all the world there was but one man meant for her and, come what may, she would do all in her power to have him. Closing her eyes, she again felt the hot sun on her face, saw the field white with daisies, felt his kiss, so tender, so full of promises to keep. Again she murmured her vow to be true to him, to never doubt him, a vow no less binding for having been unspoken.

She also remembered the barbarians clamoring outside the walls, storming the gates. *The massive wooden bar splintered, then broke with an explosive crack.* She expected to find herself swept aside, to be trampled underfoot, to be the victim of unimaginable horrors. Instead her spirits soared. She felt liberated, free at last.

When, later still, she lay in darkness savoring her memories of the afternoon, trying to prolong this special day by postponing the falling of the curtain of sleep, she remembered Old Cob. She'd been on her way to visit Old Cob and then all thoughts of the gypsy had been swept from her mind.

Tomorrow, she promised herself, tomorrow.

Chapter Nine

The next day, as Maud rode slowly away from the Twin Oaks stables, she seemed to find herself a visitor in a strange new world.

Her memories of the day before, of Lord Montrain finding her at the ruins, pursuing her on horseback, kissing her and garlanding her head with daisies, were crystal clear as though captured and placed on display beneath a bell jar. The actual world around her, on the other hand, appeared indistinct and somehow far removed; she viewed the brilliant noon-high sun, the deep blue of the sky, the scattering of white clouds, and the green of the leaves as through gauze painted a delicate rose.

When she rounded the corner of the great house and rode onto the sweep of the gravel drive, she saw Gwen sitting on a bench between the twin oaks with a drawing board on her lap and a paint box at her side. Her sister wore a becoming yellow gown, and Maud sighed, wishing fashionable colors were as kind to her as they were to Gwen.

"Maud," Gwen called, looking up at the sound of the horse, "pray come tell me what you think of my painting."

After dismounting and tethering Juno, Maud hesitated before going to her sister. Since she wanted to share the secret of the events of the day before with someone, why not with Gwen? She no longer believed Lord Montrain had kissed Gwen in the Plimsall garden. She couldn't bring herself to believe it after he'd kissed her in the field of daisies. Her heart told her she could trust him.

Yet she was reluctant to confide in Gwen, fearful her more sophisticated sister might laugh at her, calling her a feather-headed schoolgirl for trusting any man, especially one she hardly knew. Besides, Maud treasured her secret, prized it, wanted to hold it close. If she shared her precious memories, scattered them, might they not fade and shrivel like plucked flowers left too long in the sun?

No, she wouldn't tell Gwen, at least not now.

Maud looked over her sister's shoulder at the almost finished watercolor. And blinked in surprise. Gwen had almost succeeded in changing the imposing stone pile of Twin Oaks into a castle fit for a fairy-tale prince. Almost, but not quite.

In Gwen's painting, the three-story structure appeared taller and narrower than it actually was. The brick chimneys had become crenelated towers, the russet tiles covering the upper third of the house were now a bright red, and the neat, ordered English gardens had been transformed into eruptions of tropical color.

As though sensing Maud's surprise, Gwen said, "This is the way I picture Twin Oaks. Perhaps this is how I'd like it to be. At least I'd like to remember it this way."

"Your painting's charming. Enchanting." And,

Maud told herself, it was. Even though the actual Twin Oaks looked no more like the house in the watercolor than she resembled Gwen.

Maud shook her head, angry at herself. She *wasn't* a pale shadow of her older sister; why did she keep thinking of herself as one? Perhaps a year or even six months ago she might have seen herself that way, but not any longer. She wasn't a faded copy of Gwen or of anyone. She was herself. She differed from her sister, but she was not inferior. Her father had helped change her perception of herself as had Mrs. Wilcomb and M. Lusignon. And, above all, Lord Montrain.

How like Gwen, Maud thought even as she admired her sister's painting, to see only what she wanted to see and leave out all the rest, conveniently omitting the dark, the drear, and the mundane. If only she, Maud, could do the same, how much more pleasant her life would become. She was able to pretend for a time—her father often chided her for spending too much time daydreaming—but her more practical side had a rude habit of always summoning her back to everyday realities.

"All this last week," Gwen told her, "I've been painting scenes at Twin Oaks, the house, the vistas from the windows, the grotto, the obelisk, the gardens, the park, the Adam fireplace. When I'm not living here any longer, I'll be able to look at my paintings and remember you and Papa and the wonderful times we had."

Maud raised her eyebrows. "You talk as though you were about to have Papa order our traveling coach readied to transport you to some *terra incognita* at the edge of the world."

125

Gwen reddened. "Young ladies do marry and they do leave home to be with their husbands," she said. "Sometimes fate decrees that they live far from home."

With a pang, Maud recalled that Lord Montrain's ancestral estate was somewhere in distant Cornwall. How suspicious she'd become! She quickly thrust the unwelcome thought from her mind.

Gwen suddenly looked up. "Maud! Listen! Do you hear hoofbeats?"

Maud raised her head, and after a moment she heard the sound of an approaching horse. Gwen gazed expectantly at the spot where a horseman would first appear, sighing with disappointment when Mr. Robert Plimsall cantered from beneath the trees.

" 'Always get the damn kiddies off the street.' " Maud whispered.

Gwen smothered a laugh just in time to nod in response when Mr. Plimsall doffed his hat.

Every Saturday afternoon during the summer, Lord Ashley, Robert Plimsall, and two other gentlemen met for a game of whist. As he slapped his trump cards onto the table, Mr. Plimsall invariably exclaimed in a voice loud enough to be heard well beyond the card room, "Always get the damn kiddies off the street."

"You promised," Maud said as soon as Mr. Plimsall had passed by, "that when you married I would be your maid of honor."

Gwen frowned. "I did, didn't I?" she murmured as much to herself as to Maud. For a time she sat staring into the distance as though at something only she could see.

How distracted Gwen seemed of late, Maud thought.

Gwen roused herself. "And of course you shall," she promised, "and Papa will give me away." She brightened. "And then you'll marry, dear Maud, and Papa will be left to live alone here at Twin Oaks. I wouldn't be at all surprised if he marries again once he has both of us off his hands."

"How strange. I was thinking something of the sort only the other day. And Mrs. Wilcomb said the same." She lowered her voice although they were alone beneath the oaks. "The notion caught me quite unawares. I never before envisioned Papa marrying again."

"Maud, you're such a naïf. Haven't you noticed the way a great many women look at Papa? That Mrs. Comfort, for one. Not only widows, either. And haven't you seen the way he looks at them?"

"I didn't until the day of the Guildford Stakes," Maud admitted.

Gwen placed her drawing board on the bench, rose, and hugged Maud, then held her at arm's length. "How young you seem at times, dear Maud," she said, smiling. "I often wonder what will become of you when I'm not here to look after you."

Maud shook her head in an effort to rearrange her thoughts. Does Gwen actually see herself as my protector, she wondered, even now that we're both grown?

"I never offer advice," Gwen went on, "but you must be wary of men like M. Lusignon. There's something about him —" She crossed her arms and shuddered.

"I find him quite charming." Maud was surprised to hear herself defending the Frenchman. It wasn't that she particularly liked him; the truth was she tended to defend people under attack.

"As I'm certain the Devil can be whenever it suits his purposes." Gwen looked up at the house. "Even now," she said, "I can't help wondering if at this very moment he's concealed behind the curtains in one of those upper rooms, spying on the two of us. Why did he come to Twin Oaks, Maud? What does he want from us?"

"I supposed he was a friend of Papa's."

Gwen shook her head. "No, since Papa told me he never met him before he appeared at Twin Oaks, I suspect Papa doesn't know what he's after either. And tolerates him only as a favor to the Prime Minister."

"Whatever he is, M. Lusignon's hardly the Devil, nor does he behave in a particularly devilish manner. He appears strange to you, to us, because he's foreign, and so we're not accustomed to his ways." Maud was surprised to find herself taking the role of M. Lusignon's champion while at the same time sounding like a schoolmistress.

"Fiddlesticks! You must have noticed how he watches us." Gwen became earnest. "Don't trust him, Maud, no matter how skillful a dancer or how charming he may be." She returned to the bench and started to pick up her drawing board.

"Come with me," Maud said impulsively. "I'm riding to visit Old Cob at his cottage. It's not far."

Gwen glanced at the grazing Juno, grimaced, then shook her head. Finding a sponge, she dampened the unfinished corner of her watercolor.

128

4 FREE BOOKS

TO GET YOUR 4 FREE BOOKS WORTH $18.00 —MAIL IN THE FREE BOOK CERTIFICATE T O D A Y

Fill in the Free Book Certificate below, and we'll send your FREE BOOKS to you as soon as we receive it.

If the certificate is missing below, write to: Zebra Home Subscription Service, Inc., P.O. Box 5214, 120 Brighton Road, Clifton, New Jersey 07015-5214.

FREE BOOK CERTIFICATE

4 FREE BOOKS

ZEBRA HOME SUBSCRIPTION SERVICE, INC.

YES! Please start my subscription to Zebra Historical Romances and send me my first 4 books absolutely FREE. I understand that each month I may preview four new Zebra Historical Romances free for 10 days. If I'm not satisfied with them, I may return the four books within 10 days and owe nothing. Otherwise, I will pay the low preferred subscriber's price of just $3.75 each; a total of $15.00, *a savings off the publisher's price of $3.00.* I may return any shipment and I may cancel this subscription at any time. There is no obligation to buy any shipment and there are no shipping, handling or other hidden charges. Regardless of what I decide, the four free books are mine to keep.

NAME

ADDRESS _____ APT

CITY _____ STATE ZIP

(   )
TELEPHONE

SIGNATURE _____ (if under 18, parent or guardian must sign)

Terms, offer and prices subject to change without notice. Subscription subject to acceptance by Zebra Books. Zebra Books reserves the right to reject any order or cancel any subscription.

GET
FOUR
FREE
BOOKS

(AN $18.00 VALUE)

ZEBRA HOME SUBSCRIPTION
SERVICE, INC.
P.O. Box 5214
120 BRIGHTON ROAD
CLIFTON, NEW JERSEY 07015-5214

"Though I don't approve of you riding hither and thither over the countryside by yourself," she said, "I really must finish this painting today."

Maud kissed her sister quickly on the cheek, neither affronted nor surprised by Gwen's reluctance to ride with her. After mounting Juno, she considered the enticing idea of going to Old Cob's by way of the monastery but immediately dismissed the thought. Today she intended to let nothing stop her from hearing Old Cob's version of the supposed thefts at Twin Oaks.

Arriving at the gypsy's cottage after an uneventful ride, she left Juno tied in front and walked to the rear where she found Old Cob dozing in the shade of a dilapidated shed.

Though there was a hoe at his side, weeds threatened to gain the upper hand in his garden, and Maud noted with a frown of disappointment that the height of his few rows of corn lagged the crop in the Twin Oak fields by several inches. Not for the first time she wondered how he managed to feed and clothe himself. In years past she'd heard talk that he poached game, but surely he was too old for that now.

When she softly spoke his name, Old Cob opened his eyes, blinking, finally using a gnarled stick to help himself struggle to his feet. He doffed his cap to her with an exaggerated sweep of his arm. "My benefactress," he said, "Old Cob welcomes you to his humble home."

Though suspecting his mockery was meant to hide his hurt pride, she was still taken aback.

When she didn't answer, he said, "Old Cob begs your forgiveness. Ye mean no harm. He's well aware you're not one of them. Old habits, like old men, die hard, Maud."

Maud, not Lady Maud. She was aware that Old Cob refused to use titles. "When the bloody aristocracy earns Old Cob's respect," she'd overheard him say, "Old Cob'll give it to them. Not before." The only time she'd heard the word *lord* pass his lips was years ago when he'd talked of Lord Nonesuch, dead these many years. Lord Nonesuch had been Old Cob's pig.

Her father had once said, "Old Cob piles insult on top of insult, but the only one he injures is himself." Maud agreed even while grudgingly admiring the old man's defiant spirit.

"I don't mind, Bendigo," she said.

"They only come to visit Old Cob when they're wanting something," he went on. "Like last week, asking did Old Cob know a gypsy fortune teller for their Ashton Fair? Old Cob wouldn't of told them even if he had."

"I fear I want something from you, too, since I came here to talk about Ne'er-Do-Well." And the thefts at Twin Oaks, she reminded herself.

"Old Cob's always willing to talk horses. Come inside, Maud, us'll have a cuppa."

She followed him into the cottage where, vaguely ill-at-ease, she perched on the edge of a bench at a wooden table. The poorly lit room was sparsely furnished though so cluttered Maud had to resist her impulse to return dishes and discarded clothing to their rightful places.

Old Cob poured from a white porcelain teapot delicately decorated with red and blue flowers blooming amidst green leaves.

130

"How beautiful," Maud said. The teapot rivaled any she'd seen at Twin Oaks, making her wonder how the old man came by it.

" 'Twas my mother's, God rest her soul. Bow china, she called it." Old Cob sat across from her and took a sip of the hot tea. "And what of Ne'er-Do-Well?" he asked. "Talk at the Unicorn had it he fared mighty poorly at Guildford."

"He finished a lagging fifth. Vulcan won."

"Ay, Montrain's horse."

"Do you know Lord Montrain?" Maud, reasonably certain he didn't, admitted to herself she'd asked the question only to say Lord Montrain's name.

At first she thought the old man nodded but then realized his head had bobbed of its own accord. "Don't know the man," Old Cob said. "What's more, Old Cob don't care to know him." He hunched his shoulders, gripped his chin with his hand, and the trembling stopped. "And what sort of race did Ne'er-Do-Well run?"

Maud described how her horse had taken the lead at the start and held his own through most of the mile and a half only to falter nearing the finish.

When she was done, he asked, "Did Old Cob ever tell ye he saw the great Eclipse race?"

She shook her head. "I've heard Tom talk of Eclipse."

"Faugh! What Tom Whittaker knows of race horses could be put in a thimble. And still ye'd have room for your finger."

About to use his disparagement of Tom as an entree to ask about the thefts, she held back, deciding it was best to let Old Cob tell her what was on his mind first. "You saw Eclipse run," she prompted.

131

"A young man Old Cob was at the time, traveling from place to place, living by his wits. If he recollects aright, Eclipse was a five-year-old and 'twas his first season of racing. The race was all of four miles — they mostly were in those days — with Eclipse carrying fourteen stone, the weight of a full-grown man. He won, Eclipse did, for wasn't he the grandest horse ever to see the light of day in England? 'Eclipse first,' they used to say, 'the rest nowhere.' "

"I don't understand how this concerns Ne'er-Do-Well."

"Why, didn't ye know? Eclipse is his forebear some five or six generations back. 'Tis not the fact of Eclipse winning race after race, 'tis the how of it. He laid back, biding his time for mile after mile, letting the others tire, then in the last three furlongs he called on his courage, passing the other horses, one and all, as if they was standing still."

"You mean Ne'er-Do-Well should wait until the end of the race to try for the lead? But Tom says — "

"The hell with what Tom says. Begging your pardon, Maud." He drank the last of his tea. When he put the empty cup on the table, she winced to notice that his hand shook uncontrollably.

"Old Cob's always maintained," he went on, "if one thing don't work, you should try something else. Where has listening to Tom Whittaker ever got Ne'er-Do-Well? I'll tell ye where. Finishing the Guildford stakes with four other horses ahead of him, that's where."

"Your suggestion might be worth trying," Maud admitted. "Yet how can we be sure?"

Old Cob raised his hands. "There's nothing sure in this life save that one day we'll all reach the end of it. And that the rich, base and vile as some may be, get richer while the poor get poorer."

"Not the rich who wagered on Ne'er-Do-Well." Realizing she had to shift the subject back to the training of her horse or risk listening to a lecture she'd heard before, Maud hurriedly said, "Perhaps you could watch Ne'er-Do-Well run. That might tell you if we should change our tactics."

"Old Cob's obligated to ye, Maud, for letting him live out his life in this cottage. And he likes ye, besides. He'll watch your horse run. Tomorrow?"

The next day was Sunday with church services in the morning and a visit to the Athertons planned for the afternoon. "The day after tomorrow?" she suggested.

"Ten in the morning? At Twin Oaks? In the east meadow?" When Maud nodded, Old Cob said, "Good."

"Tom will have to ride Ne'er-Do-Well."

Old Cob shrugged. "The man rides well enough. 'Tis when it comes to thinking he's lacking."

This was her chance to bring up the matter of the long-ago thefts. "When I was little," she said, "I remember Tom having a son who helped in the stables at Twin Oaks."

"Ay, and a regular devil was young Tom. Old Cob was gone from Twin Oaks by then, but he heard tell the last straw came when his father caught the lad pinching coins from his mother's purse. Whipped the boy something fierce, he did. The next day young Tom took hisself off to London and never come back."

So she'd been right, young Tom had been the thief! "And yet my father thought you'd been stealing when all the time it must have been young Tom. Couldn't you have told him the way it was?"

Old Cob folded his arms across his chest. "If the west wind blew across Twin Oaks sending the air onto Plimsall land, your father'd send a passel of his servants to try to catch it and bring it back."

Maud stared at him, confused. "Air? I'm afraid I don't understand."

"There's certain things put on this earth for the good of all. Needful things, the air we breathe for one, the trees in the woods, the fish in the streams, the fowl of the fields, the game in the forests. A man can't nail up a warning sign or plant a hedge fence and say whatever's on this side is mine. Some things belong to everybody, rich and poor alike."

What was Old Cob trying to tell her? Then, with a sinking heart, she understood his meaning, or thought she did. "You did take something from Twin Oaks," she said.

"Maybe a chicken or two when Old Cob was hungry, he and his. Do the gentry expect poor men and women to starve, to have their young 'uns roam the lanes begging when the gentry's got nothing better to do than to be leering and sniggering at old Plimsall's snuffboxes?"

Maud felt her face flush with embarrassment since she knew what Old Cob's meant. Georgie Plimsall himself had hinted to Gwen that certain of his father's French snuffboxes, the ones kept in a locked cabinet, had indelicate pictures engraved on the backs of their lids. She couldn't quite fathom, though, why Old Cob thought Robert Plimsall's owning indecent snuffboxes was a justification for stealing chickens from Twin Oaks.

134

Old Cob had always talked as though he wanted to rend the fabric of English society, lay waste to civilization as they knew it, and start over again, although she'd never heard him explain how he intended to rebuild what he had destroyed. Her father, on the other hand, was content with things as they were, as well he and other landowners might well be. She saw her own ideas falling somewhere in between the two men, for she believed change was necessary but that it should come slowly with each person making his or her contribution to progress, small and insignificant though it might seem at the time.

"And where once a man could snare a rabbit or an otter, and no harm done to anyone," Old Cob said, "now the gentry's got their mantraps set and their spring guns loaded, waiting to maim or kill ye."

So Old Cob had stolen from Twin Oaks, just what her father had claimed. And she'd refused to believe. Disappointed, Maud frowned and shook her head. She'd been sailing confidently along, trusting the fresh wind at her back to bring her safely to port. Now, suddenly, the wind had died, leaving her becalmed.

Old Cob touched her sleeve with a hand misshapen by rheumatism. "Don't fret so, young Maud," he told her. "Ye'll find men can't help being what they are. Changing them's a task for a saint, not a maid like yourself."

Anyone could always change if they wanted to, she told herself. What hope was there for the world if they couldn't?

But a short while later, as she rode slowly back to

Twin Oaks, she asked herself how she could have been so wrong about Old Cob. Not that she no longer liked him, she did, but he'd disappointed her. By being himself, she supposed. The warning signs had been there if only she hadn't been too blind to see them. She'd known Old Cob had poached in years past. And she'd been aware of the casual way gypsies treated the private property of others.

If she'd been wrong about Old Cob, was she also mistaken about others? About Lord Montrain, for one? She'd known Old Cob for years, albeit not well, while she'd met Montrain only a few weeks ago. Even in that short time she'd noticed warning signs, his recklessness, his ambivalence, but had, until now, chosen to ignore them.

Why couldn't life be simple? she wondered.

She urged Juno on, unable to dispel her growing uneasiness, her many misgivings. If life were simple, she consoled herself, it wouldn't be nearly as interesting. Besides, didn't her heart tell her that Lord Montrain loved her even though she suspected he might not have admitted that fact to himself?

As she rode from under the trees and caught sight of home, she noticed that Gwen was no longer seated beneath the oaks, then she glimpsed a flash of yellow off to her right. Slowing Juno, she peered between the trees in the park. Again the yellow appeared only to disappear almost at once, and she realized it must be a rider leaving Twin Oaks on the same path Maud had followed the day before when she returned from the monastery.

Gwen had been wearing a yellow gown while she painted her watercolor. Gwen, she realized now, had behaved as though she'd been expecting someone. A messenger?

Maud swung Juno from the roadway, urged her between the rows of trees, and reined the mare onto the path, prodding her into a lope. When she reached the top of a small rise, Maud was able to look ahead where she saw the yellow-gowned rider sitting stiffly upright in her sidesaddle.

It was Gwen. She could hardly credit what she saw, but there was no doubt of it. Her sister, who normally shunned riding, who insisted on the appropriate dress for each occasion, had not only mounted a horse and ridden away from Twin Oaks by herself, but hadn't even paused long enough to change into a riding habit.

Maud followed along the path despite a twinge of guilt. Though she admitted she might be spying on her sister, she told herself she had to discover the truth.

At first she was careful to lag well behind, but when she saw Gwen was in such a hurry or else so unsure of her riding ability that she never looked back, Maud increased her pace. As she rode on, she experienced despair, of being caught up in dire events over which she had no control, as though, adrift in a river's fast-flowing current, she was being drawn inexorably toward the lip of a mighty falls.

For it was evident that Gwen was on her way to Blackstone House.

Maud followed her, blinking back tears as she rode across the field of daisies, followed her through the dark tunnel of the grove. Instead of veering up the hill to the monastery ruins, Gwen hastened directly to the London road, staying on the road for less than a mile before turning again to ride between the pillars and past the gatehouse at the entrance to Blackstone House.

Maud rode along the rutted drive until the house came into view, a massive dark structure with four equally massive chimneys in the front. Both house and grounds appeared deserted. Maud slowed and watched Gwen ride to the side of the house, slide down from the saddle, and run toward a door partially concealed by overgrown shrubbery.

Maud guided Juno into the woods, an ill-kept park with underbrush proliferating under the trees, and reined in. Turning, she was in time to see Gwen raise her hand and tap on the door. Within moments, as though someone had been expecting her, the door swung open, and Maud glimpsed Lord Montrain. She gave a cry of pain.

Lord Montrain held his arms out to Gwen, she went to him, the door closed.

Chapter Ten

That evening Lord Ashley entertained his fellow whist players and M. Lusignon at a sumptuous dinner of oysters, roast lamb, and pheasant.

Gwen arrived late, murmuring apologies to her father and his guests, smiling tentatively at Maud. She looked radiant in a high-waisted coral gown, its square neckline edged with white ruffles. All during the meal, Maud noticed, the gentlemen stole admiring glances at her sister while they talked desultorily of the weather, shooting, and the low price of corn. Maud said little, distracted both by her suspicion that Lord Montrain had betrayed her and a dull throbbing in her head.

Following a dessert of grape pudding and cream rolls, Mrs. Wilcomb excused herself, and the gentlemen retired to enjoy cigars and madeira. Only then did Maud have an opportunity to speak to Gwen.

"When I was returning from Old Cob's," she said, "I was surprised to see you riding away from Twin Oaks."

Gwen glanced quickly about, then answered in a low voice, "This has been one of the most memorable days of my life. A wonderful day." She covered Maud's hand with her own. "Don't question me, dear Maud. Though I learned many things today, I promised not to speak a word of them yet, not even to you."

Maud stared at her sister, a score of questions in her mind demanding answers, but she said nothing, finally turning away and lowering her head so Gwen wouldn't see her eyes misting. The pain in her head grew worse, threatening to develop into a serious attack of the megrims.

Gwen rose and put her hand on Maud's arm. "I love you, dear Maud," she whispered. "I love everyone in the whole world." After a pause, she added, "Except for M. Lusignon. I don't care a fig for him."

Maud heard the rustle of Gwen's gown, and when she looked up, she found herself alone in the dining room. Rising slowly, she left the dining room to wander aimlessly along the vast echoing hall with its Belgian tapestries and suits of armor. She glanced into the library, but the row upon row of leather spines spoke to her not of life but of dull and tedious imitations. As she returned along the hall, the murmur of talk and laughter coming from the gentlemen in the smoking room caused her to feel more alone than ever.

One cup of Mrs. Wilcomb's tisanes, she told herself, might help ease the pounding in her head. Or should she retire to her darkened bedchamber and try to find relief in sleep? Or perhaps the evening air would provide the remedy she sought.

Maud left the house by way of the French doors in the drawing room, finding that the lowering sun was sending slanting rays through the trees. A fresh breeze caressed her face as she listlessly made her way into the garden where not even the sweet, nostalgic scent of honeysuckle could enliven her spirits.

For some reason Lord Montrain's face flashed across her inner vision, his brown eyes glowing as they had when he'd held her in his arms in the field of daisies. A disquieting warmth blossomed inside her, but a warmth that quickly yielded to a yearning followed by despair.

Sitting on a bench under a rose arbor, she sighed despondently but then, reminding herself that, though it might feel to her as though the world had ended with her discovery of Gwen's rendezvous at Blackstone House, the truth was that the sun still shone, the breeze blew, and the roses twining above her head smelled as sweet as ever. The world went on and so must she. Somehow.

The first step was to discover the truth.

Sitting up straight, she drew in a deep breath, her mind made up. If Gwen wouldn't confide in her, and evidently her sister had decided not to, she'd have to go to Lord Montrain himself for an explanation of his conduct. How she could possibly arrange to do so within the bounds of propriety she didn't know, but do it she would. And soon.

"May I join you, Lady Maud?"

Startled, she looked up to find M. Lusignon, dressed in black except for his burgundy waistcoat and a snow-white shirt and cravat, standing a few feet from her holding a long, thin cigar in his hand. "I'll gladly extinguish my cigar if it antagonizes you," he said.

Maud, thankful for the distraction, shook her

141

head, noting that while M. Lusignon spoke excellent English, his choice of words, at times, rang discordantly in her ears.

He sat on a marble bench opposite her, his curly black hair glistening in the last of the sunlight. "The discussions in the smoking room of the price of Surrey corn and the preferred method to play a difficult hand of whist grew tiresome," he said. "To be truthful, I'd much prefer to talk inconsequential nonsense with a beautiful young lady such as yourself than have a spirited intellectual exchange with the most learned and witty of gentlemen."

And what young lady preferred to sit in a garden alone rather than listen to compliments from a gentleman even if she knew, that particular gentleman would never be the love of her life?

"Am I to understand," she asked, "that you find my conversation inconsequential nonsense?"

"*Touché!* You've succeeded in skewering me with my own opening conversational gambit." He leaned toward her. "Did your father inform you I've been asked to perform an exhibition with the rapier at Ashton Fair? The word of my fencing skill has spread even to Surrey, it seems." He smiled as though to excuse his boasting. "I only hope I don't ever have to cross swords with you, Lady Maud."

"I'd never be a match for you, M. Lusignon, either with swords or with words." A sudden surge of pain in her temples made her shudder and put a hand to her forehead.

"I suspected at dinner you were suffering from *mal de tête*. What do you English say, headache?"

Even her slight nod made her head pound.

"Perhaps I can be of some assistance," M. Lusignon said. "My father was a physician in Paris where he practiced with Franz Mesmer, an Austrian. Dr. Mesmer discovered a healing force he chose to call animal magnetism. Even Benjamin Franklin, the American, was impressed with the many cures he achieved."

"He didn't use medicines? Or leeches for bleeding?"

"Sparingly if at all. Since so much of illness proceeds from the mind and not from the body, he harnessed the power of suggestion to effect his cures. As it happens, when I resided in Fort-de-France on the Caribbean island of Martinique, I had the opportunity to experiment with Dr. Mesmer's methods. Achieving a certain degree of success, I might add."

Extinguishing his cigar, M. Lusignon removed a gold watch from his pocket. "If you will permit me, Lady Maud, I shall give you a brief demonstration. Nothing is required of you except that you observe my watch."

He let the watch swing slowly back and forth on its gold chain. "Listen to me while you think of nothing," he told her in a low, soothing voice, "nothing at all."

Maud saw no harm in doing what he asked. As he talked on and on, his words blurred in her mind, growing fainter and fainter until they were like pleasant music heard from afar. She was floating, rocked gently by water lapping around her. Her breathing deepened; she was at peace in a world of gentle serenity.

143

Maud roused with a start. Had she been asleep? She must have dozed off because here was M. Lusignon sitting next to her, his brown eyes inches from hers. His nearness didn't disturb her because she trusted him. He meant no harm to her or hers—he was her dear friend.

"The ache in your head?" he asked.

"Why, the megrim's completely gone. I feel wonderful." Almost giddy, she thought with flicker of surprise.

"You're an excellent patient." He drew back, pocketing his gold watch. "I merely suggested to you that your ache in the head should depart and, *voilá,* depart it did."

"How strange that I don't remember," she said. "But I'm most grateful to you. Why, you could be a great healer."

M. Lusignon shook his head. "So much depends on the patient, Lady Maud. My powers are successful only with a few, and they alleviate only a limited number of ailments. Your father's gout, I fear, would be quite impervious to my ministrations. At one time, however, I did consider becoming a physician but decided I had even greater skills in other regions."

While awed by M. Lusignon's abilities, she couldn't help being amused by his high opinion of himself. So far he'd admitted to being an expert swordsman and a skilled healer. What other talents did he possess? She was certain she'd soon be told.

"I'm impressed, M. Lusignon," she told him.

He let a nod serve as his acknowledgement of her compliment. "Some have maintained I too often boast of my accomplishments. If I have the guilt, it is only because I adhere to a code of absolute truth. Would you have me speak falsehoods to appear modest in the eyes of the world?"

She couldn't help smiling.

"Did I say something droll?" he asked. "At times I am inadvertently amusing by means of my choice of English words. Since I speak five languages fluently and read eight, on occasion my words become less than precise."

Maud hadn't meant to hurt his feelings, so she sought a way to soothe any pain she might have caused him. "I didn't mean to laugh at you. I've never met anyone quite like you, M. Lusignon, and sometimes when I'm unsure of myself or confused, I hide it by smiling."

Cocking his head slightly to one side, he traced the outline of the right half of his moustache with his finger. "I have observed that about you," he said. "In fact, my greatest talent is for observing and interpreting the actions of others."

Maud looked quickly at him, remembering how Gwen suspected he watched her comings and goings, how she herself often had the uncomfortable feeling he was watching her.

"I can see from your glance that you've noticed me observing others; the more perceptive do, I regret to say, no matter how unobtrusive I attempt to remain. I began exploring the behavior of my fellow humans to agreeably pass the time when I resided for a few years in Dakar in West Africa since, as you might imagine, a Frenchman finds few sources of amusement in Dakar. My talent for observing

145

developed from my interest in phrenology."

At least she knew what the word meant. "Isn't that the prediction of a person's character by studying the shape of his head?"

"Precisely. Since one of my lesser duties in Dakar was to hire servants for the governor-general, I decided to use my knowledge of phrenology to eliminate undesirable applicants. Those whose head shapes indicated they were overly greedy, for example. My faith in phrenology was shaken when the first houseboy I employed made off with most of the governor-general's finest silver."

At least, she thought, M. Lusignon didn't believe he was perfect. She shouldn't, though, be secretly laughing at him; he might notice and be hurt. Besides, one shouldn't laugh at a dear friend.

"Following several other thefts by the servants," he went on, "I was transferred to Algiers where I became aide to the French consul. At about the same time, I abandoned phrenology to perfect my powers of observation. So I began watching others, noting how they responded to events in the world around them. I became so successful I had the honor of assisting Marshal Ney during his Austrian campaign by questioning enemy prisoners at El-chingen."

He'd lived in so many places, Maud thought, he'd done so many unusual things, while she had scarcely ventured beyond London and Surrey. That, though, didn't mean she hadn't used her own powers of observation. "Sometimes," she said, "I can tell what someone's thinking by the look in his eyes."

146

"There are those who believe the eyes reveal the soul. As for myself, I direct my attention mainly to the lips, whether they turn down in displeasure or up in happiness, for example. And to the hands. When I first spoke to you a few minutes ago, you clasped your hands together in your lap as though you distrusted me. Now, happily, your hands tell me quite a different story."

Maud glanced down at her hands, one on each side of her on the bench. He was right, her feelings toward him had changed. Remarkable!

"My powers proved rather useful to my government during the Congress of Vienna where M. Talleyrand requested me to observe certain of the other delegates."

M. Lusignon smiled reminiscently. "You would have loved Vienna, Lady Maud," he said, "and I would have enjoyed showing the city to you. Vienna was thronged with visitors. There were promenades, dancing, beautifully gowned women with their dazzling jewels, plays and operas, and, after a January snow, torchlit processions of sledges going to the Palace of Schonbrunn to watch a performance of *Cinderella*."

She would have loved to have been in Vienna during the Congress, riding in a sleigh, bells jingling, the snow sparkling in the light from the torches. One of her dreams was to travel, to see France, Italy, the Alps, the West Indies. Anywhere and everywhere in the world.

"I perceive from your expression that I'm right about Vienna," he said. "May I offer a suggestion, Lady Maud? You should never become a spy, although you'd be a charming one, for your face can't help but reveal your innermost thoughts."

She drew in a deep breath, consciously removing all expression from her face while turning her mind into a blank slate. "And what are my innermost thoughts at this moment?" she challenged him.

He smiled. "Perhaps you're wondering why someone who has seen so much of the world, as I have, and is able to travel where he wishes, as I am, is presently residing in your English county of Surrey."

"The question has crossed my mind since I never took you for a diner-out."

"Did you ever consider that Surrey might be as exotic for a Frenchman as, say, the isles of Greece or the River Nile is for an Englishman?"

"No, I never did." She looked directly into his dark eyes. "And I don't for one minute believe you find Surrey exotic, M. Lusignon."

"I must admit you're quite right." The smile left his face. "The reason I'm here at Twin Oaks is to attempt to discover if Mr. Philip Faurot is in reality M. Guy Gournay."

Maud's eyes widened as she drew in a shocked breath. "You think Mr. Faurot is an imposter?"

"Precisely, Lady Maud. I suspect he is, but as of now I have no proof."

"But why would he pose as someone he's not?"

"The circumstances leading to his assuming a false identity are much too sordid for your tender ears."

"My ears aren't as tender as you might believe," she said tartly, still trying to come to terms with his suspicions concerning Philip Faurot. "Besides, I

148

doubt if you would have mentioned the deception if you didn't intend to tell me about it."

"You *are* perceptive. Yes, you should be made aware of my reasons for suspecting him if only to prevent yourself or someone close to you from becoming another of this man's victims." M. Lusignon stroked his moustache before going on. "The infamous deeds of which I speak," he said, "occurred for the most part in New Orleans, one city where I have never been. Therefore I can only repeat what I've been told by reputable persons.

"M. Guy Gournay," he went on, "and, I believe, his father fled from France to avoid service in Napoleon's army. After settling in New Orleans, Philip soon acquired a reputation for being what you English call 'a ladies' man,' carelessly making protestations of love to young women and then soon after leaving them for a sweeter flower. One of his abandoned loves, Angelique, became so distraught by his betrayal that she drowned herself."

Maud bit her lip. "How terrible."

"Exactly. This Guy Gournay is a most despicable example of French manhood. Besides broken hearts, he left one gentleman dead and another maimed after they challenged him to duels. I, Maurice Lusignon, have vowed to find this M. Gournay and kill him."

Rendered momentarily speechless, Maud stared at M. Lusignon. "But has he harmed you?" she asked finally.

M. Lusignon sighed and lowered his eyes. "Angelique, a woman so gay, so alive, was my sister," he said in a voice choked with emotion. "Guy Gournay murdered her as surely as if he'd shot her with one of his dueling pistols."

Feeling her eyes prick with tears, Maud impulsively covered his hand with hers. "I'm so very sorry," she told him. "I don't think I could abide it if anything ever happened to my sister, to Gwen."

"I was confident you'd understand." He raised her hand to his lips and kissed it. "Forgive me," he said, "if I appear overly bold. Your kindness has overwhelmed me."

Flustered, Maud withdrew her hand, unable to think of anything to say. While she liked and sympathized with M. Lusignon's sorrow and was fascinated by his worldly ways, she felt no tenderness toward him. M. Lusignon was her dear friend, but he would never be more. She loved one man, that one man was Lord Montrain, and she could never love another.

"When an informant in America wrote me some months ago," M. Lusignon went on, "that Guy Gournay had left New Orleans to journey to France by way of England, I set out to find him. I suspect Mr. Faurot and Gournay are one and the same man, but I'm not yet certain since I've never set eyes on the man and have received only a vague description. I do know, however, that M. Gournay suffered a wound to his right shoulder in one of his duels that left him with a scar in the form of an X."

She asked the question that had been nagging her ever since M. Lusignon revealed the reason for his presence in Surrey. "And what does Lord Montrain have to do with all this?"

M. Lusignon shrugged. "My informant made no mention of Lord Montrain, and as you're aware, messages take weeks to travel across the Atlantic to America and weeks more before the answers make their way back here to England. There are many possibilities: Lord Montrain may be unaware of his friend's notorious past; he may be choosing to ignore it for reasons of his own; Mr. Faurot may have influence over him and is using it to force him to lend a cachet to his activities; or I could be mistaken and Mr. Faurot may not be Guy Gournay at all. But enough of this sordid subject. I regret the necessity of having burdened you with it. Come inside with me, Lady Maud, I have something to show you."

He led her into the house, along the hall, and then across the drawing room to the large oval looking glass on the wall. She watched him in the mirror while, standing behind her, he took a velvet pouch from his pocket, opened it, and held aloft a diamond necklace.

"Ever since I arrived at Twin Oaks, I've wanted to see how this looks on you," he said, fastening it around her neck before she could protest.

Maud drew in her breath in awe as she gazed at the reflection of the diamonds sparkling in the candlelight. Even worn over her white high-necked gown of French muslin, the jewels took her breath away.

"They're magnificent," she told him.

"The necklace was my mother's," he said, "and her mother's before her. It's been handed from generation to generation of the Lusignon family for more than two hundred years."

How beautiful they would look, Maud thought, worn with a ball gown, the diamonds brilliant against her fair skin.

"You were meant to wear jewels such as these," M. Lusignon said as he removed the necklace and slipped it into his pocket.

Maud wondered why he'd shown her the diamonds. He hadn't actually violated the proprieties, at least she didn't think he had since he hadn't offered her the jewels as a gift. Was he suggesting they could be hers? No, she didn't think so, but she couldn't be certain of anything having to do with M. Lusignon.

Still the incident disturbed her.

"Before I bid you good night," M. Lusignon said, "I offer you a word of caution. Some men have a habit of speaking falsely to women; the more beautiful the woman, the greater number of falsehoods they're likely to hear. Therefore, you especially should be on your guard."

Since she knew she wasn't beautiful, was M. Lusignon doing exactly what he was warning her about? "Are you suggesting you might have lied to me?" she asked.

"Not at all, my dear friend. You'll discover in time that everything I've told you is true. There are those, however, who might not be so careful with the truth."

She shook her head, not wanting to hear more. "No," she told him, "I refuse to be so cynical. I don't believe men lie to me, not about important things." She did trust Lord Montrain, she assured

152

herself, despite her nagging doubts.

"You're a true romantic, Lady Maud. I can't help but be impressed. I salute you." He bowed over her hand, turned, and left the room.

Maud stared after him, troubled and confused. She had no reason not to believe what he'd told her of Philip Faurot probably being an imposter, and yet something deep within her balked at trusting him completely. Even if he were her dear friend.

She walked to the library where she removed *Decline and Fall* from the shelf. When the book fell open to the daisies she'd pressed between the pages, she looked down wistfully at the once-vibrant flowers, now flattened and lifeless.

In the world's eyes, the diamonds she'd so briefly worn were of great value, the flowers worthless, yet in her heart she prized these daisies above all the jewels in the world.

Chapter Eleven

The Reverend Charles Findlay opened the large Bible on the pulpit to Corinthians. Instead of reading the familiar text, he intoned it from memory:

"When I was a child, I spake as a child, I understood as a child, I thought as a child: but when I became a man, I put away childish things.

"For now we see through a glass, darkly; but then face to face: now I know in part; but then shall I know even as also I am known.

"And now abideth faith, hope, charity, these three; but the greatest of these is charity."

Maud Hawthorn, sitting in the Ashley pew at the front of the church with her father, Gweneth, and Mrs. Wilcomb, closed her eyes as the Reverend Findlay began his sermon. She wasn't praying, however, nor were her thoughts at all religious.

These three, faith, hope and charity, she repeated. Did she possess all of them where Lord Montrain was concerned? Her faith in him had most assuredly been shaken, yet not destroyed; her hope was that he could explain away his seemingly aberrant behavior. As for charity—the Reverend Findlay was now explaining that charity meant love—wasn't that the emotion she felt for Lord Montrain?

How could she entertain such profane thoughts during the Sunday sermon? She'd make amends, she silently promised herself and God. Tonight she'd say twice as many prayers as was her custom and, tomorrow morning, she'd begin her oft-postponed reading of the Bible from beginning to end, from Genesis to Revelations.

Before this day was done, she knew, she'd have at least one more sin to atone for since she planned to tell a falsehood. Instead of accompanying her father and sister to visit the Athertons, she meant to plead a bad attack of the megrims so she could remain at Twin Oaks.

Which is precisely what she did.

From her bedchamber window she watched Walters drive her father's carriage along the drive on its way to the London road and the Athertons. Turning from the window, she had Agnes help her change from her gray silk church-going gown into a pink and white cotton afternoon dress, donned a straw bonnet trimmed with pink ribbons, and drew on long white gloves.

Impatient, yet realizing she must let a respectable amount of time pass before proceeding with the next step of her plan, she paced back and forth in her room until she heard the clock in the hall strike the half-hour.

After a final glance in her cheval glass, she went downstairs where she found Mrs. Wilcomb working on her embroidery in the morning room.

"My megrim's quite gone," Maud announced to

the older woman, "and so I've asked Tom to have the phaeton ready for us in fifteen minutes." Though she hadn't seen M. Lusignon since breakfast, she glanced about her before going on in a low voice. "I thought we might visit Lady Montrain, Lord Montrain's mother, at Blackstone House."

Mrs. Wilcomb raised her eyebrows. "Lady Montrain? You've not so much as exchanged cards with her so far as I know."

As she mentally chalked another sin on her already overcrowded slate, Maud said, "While we were chatting at the Plimsalls' ball, Lady Montrain invited me to call on her." Lord Montrain's mother would have, Maud assured herself, if she had been given the opportunity.

"Do you realize," Mrs. Wilcomb asked, laying aside her embroidery, "that in all the years I've lived at Twin Oaks, I've never been inside Blackstone House? Not once. The old earl used Blackstone for his shooting and hunting, but as you know it's been closed ever since he died. I'd hoped his son would entertain once he opened the house again this spring, but he hasn't. Not that he should do so merely to please me."

Mrs. Wilcomb stood up and retrieved her cane. "Blackstone House *does* have a fireplace I'd love to see."

"Good, then it's settled." Maud had been confident Mrs. Wilcomb's curiosity would overcome any hesitation she might have about accepting an invitation that was tenuous at best.

When Tom brought the phaeton to the door, Maud thanked him and took the reins—she wanted as few people as possible to know of their destination — and drove around the sweep of the Twin Oaks drive. Though she sensed someone watching them, she overcame her impulse to turn her head to look back at the upper windows of the house.

A short time later as they drove between the pillars and up the curving road to Blackstone House, Mrs. Wilcomb said, "What a charming gatehouse and what a pity to let it stand vacant."

Maud was surprised and dismayed to see the neglected condition of house and grounds. The day before, when she'd followed Gwen, she'd been preoccupied, but now she noted that saplings and brush had been allowed to multiply in the park on either side of the road, weeds threatened to drive the flowers from the gardens, and creeper grew unchecked up the sides of Blackstone House itself.

No one hurried down the steps to take their horse's reins, so Maud tethered the mare to a rusting hitching post and helped Mrs. Wilcomb from the phaeton. They climbed the steps and stopped in front of the imposing door. The house itself was silent.

Mrs. Wilcomb laid a hand on Maud's arm. "Perhaps we should come back another day," she suggested.

"Nonsense." Maud lifted the iron knocker and let it fall, hearing the sound echo hollowly within the house. When, after a long minute, no one came to answer the door, she knocked again.

The door opened and an old man peered at them from the gloom of the hallway.

Maud handed him her calling card. The butler, if

such he was, stared at it. "I'm Lady Maud Hawthorn," she told him, "and this is Mrs. Wilcomb. We're here to pay our respects to Lady Montrain."

The butler cleared his throat. "Her ladyship's returned to Seacliff House," he said. "In Cornwall."

Maud drew in her breath in surprise. She'd assumed Lord Montrain's mother was here permanently even though no one had ever told her so.

"We'd best go," Mrs. Wilcomb whispered.

Having come this far, Maud was determined not to be turned away. "Is Lord Montrain at home?" she asked.

The butler hesitated, then opened the door so they could enter. "This way," Maud thought he said as he led them along an uncarpeted hall containing no furnishings whatsoever. After opening the door to a small sitting room and seeing them inside, the butler cleared his throat once more, said, "Wait here," and shuffled away.

Though the day was sunny, the room was dark. Looking at the high narrow windows, Maud discovered the reason: the vines of the creeper had covered most of the lower panes. The room was furnished with occasional chairs, a settee, and several tables in a variety of styles, the larger pieces resting on clawed feet. On one of the smaller tables, chessmen were arranged on a board in an end game. Looking down at the pieces, she recalled that Gwen had asked their father to teach her to play chess.

She studied the position of the men. If white's

bishop attacked, she decided, he'd trap the black king. Idly, she moved the bishop diagonally across the board.

"How extraordinary!"

Maud whirled at the sound of Mrs. Wilcomb's exclamation to discover that the older woman had opened the door to the next room. Coming to look over her shoulder, Maud gave a gasp of surprise. The chairs, the tables, even the fireplace of the drawing room were all covered with white Holland cloth.

"May I help you?" Lord Montrain's voice, coming from behind her, was uninviting.

As she turned to face him, Maud felt herself blushing with embarrassment. What pries she and Mrs. Wilcomb must seem. "Mrs. Wilcomb wanted to see the fireplace," she said. How foolish she sounded!

Without a word, Lord Montrain strode past them, flung the connecting door all the way open, crossed the room to the hearth, and yanked off the cloth. The fireplace featured twin columns supporting a marble mantel. "Come into the room," he said. "How can you see from there?"

They took a few hesitant steps toward him.

"This fireplace represents an outstanding example of the Adam style," he told them in the monotonous tones of a bored lecturer. "Note the Roman influence in the columns, the graceful curves, the griffins featured in the mantelpiece."

Mrs. Wilcomb nodded, seemingly oblivious to Lord Montrain's displeasure. "I've never before beheld so charming a fireplace. It's exactly what I want in my own house if I ever have one. Do you mind terribly if I sit here for a few moments? I'd like to be able to remember the details."

"Beauty is meant to be admired." Lord Montrain removed the cover from a chair, carried the chair to within a few feet of the fireplace, and escorted Mrs. Wilcomb to it. Turning to Maud, he took her arm and led her, none too gently, into the sitting room, closing the door behind them.

He held her at arms' length. "What are you doing here?" he demanded.

"Your mother," she began. "We came to visit—"

"My mother never invited you to Blackstone House. I know that for a fact."

Again her face flamed. "Please let me go," she said, trying to make her tone as icy as his.

He dropped his arms to his sides. His brown eyes glittered with anger, the set lines of his jaw spoke of danger and something more, something that both frightened and stirred her. She wanted to lash out at him; why then did she at the same time want to fling herself into his arms?

She did neither. Instead, she walked quickly away from him to the window as she struggled to restore her composure. "The creeper should be pruned," she told him.

"Damn the creeper. Tell me why you came here today."

Tears gathered in her eyes. "I came to see you." Lord Montrain didn't answer, so she turned to him. He took a step toward her. He misunderstood her meaning, she told herself. "Because of Gwen," she said.

"Gwen?" He sounded genuinely puzzled.

"Yesterday." Angry and hurt, her words came in a rush. "I followed Gwen yesterday. She rode here to Blackstone House. To you."

Lord Montrain drew in a long breath and let it out with an exasperated sigh. "Yesterday you followed your sister here, now you've returned this afternoon. You appear to have developed a penchant for meddling in affairs that don't concern you. On the day I surprised you up at the ruins, you were spying on me, weren't you?"

Miserable yet refusing to be contrite, she shook her head.

He suddenly frowned as though a thought had occurred to him. "I wouldn't be surprised if Lusignon put you up to this," he said.

"I'm not at M. Lusignon's beck and call," she said angrily. "Though he has been watching Blackstone House from the ruins." As soon as she spoke, she felt a stab of guilt at her betrayal of M. Lusignon. "At least I think he has."

"He has, there's no doubt. I'm well aware of it and have been for weeks. Has he been up to any other mischief?"

She shook her head. "He did tell me he's been asked to give a fencing exhibition at Ashton Fair."

"You and Lusignon seem to have become rather well acquainted during these last few days."

Was that jealousy she detected in Lord Montrain's voice? She suppressed a sudden smile of satisfaction, impetuously deciding she'd give him a wee bit more to be jealous about. "M. Lusignon and I had a delightful conversation only last evening," she said

161

blithely. "He's traveled all over the world, he's a healer and very knowledgeable and a gentleman and, besides, he's my dear friend."

"What a remarkable individual the Frenchman must be! And did I hear you aright? You and he are dear friends as well?"

Somehow the words sounded wrong coming from Lord Montrain, suggesting dark-of-night indiscretions. Defiantly, Maud raised her chin. "Yes, we are," she told him.

"I'm astounded." He smiled one-sidedly. "Not at M. Lusignon—nothing that villain says or does could surprise me since he has a reputation of being a consummate liar. It's you, Maud, M. Lusignon's dear friend Maud, you're the one who surprises me. You've acquired a sophistication of a sort since that day I saw you swinging on a vine in the glen."

Don't blush, she told herself. Whatever you do, you must not blush. To her surprise and satisfaction, she didn't.

Looking Lord Montrain in the eye, she said sweetly, "And as for you, my dear Lord Montrain, unfortunately you've acquired neither sophistication nor good manners since the day I watched you swinging on that selfsame vine."

She'd vowed to herself not to reveal she'd seen him in the glen. It was his fault she'd spoken—he'd goaded the truth out of her.

He stared at her; he blinked; his mouth opened as if to reply, but, though she waited expectantly, he said nothing. After a long moment he put his head back and roared with laughter.

She couldn't help smiling. She put her hand to

her mouth to hide the smile. Too late, his laugh was so infectious she had to laugh along with him. How foolish, how like quarreling little children the two of them were!

"Maud," he said, shaking his head. "Dear Maud, how wonderful you are. Each time I see you, you manage to delight me all over again."

He strode across the room toward her, but she stepped away until she felt the low arm of the settee against the back of her leg. He might profess to think her wonderful, even delightful, yet only minutes before he'd accused her of being a meddler and an agent of M. Lusignon while, she noticed, he'd said nothing whatsoever to explain his rendezvous with Gwen here at Blackstone House. Was he trifling with her affections?

Lord Montrain came nearer until only a whisper separated them. All at once he took her into his arms, his hands moving up her back as he drew her to him. With a startled gasp she put her hands on his chest to push him away, but he was too strong. With one hand he pulled her bonnet's ribbon, untying the bow, then lifted the bonnet from her head and tossed it to one side, releasing her dark ringlets.

He leaned forward, murmuring her name, making her pulses pound. She knew he meant to kiss her. Did he imagine he could get around her so easily? Again she tried to escape, but his fingers closed on her nape, and his lips sought hers. She leaned backwards. He leaned toward her in pursuit. She leaned farther back.

And tumbled over the arm of the settee. Instinctively she grasped him, held to him, and together they sprawled onto the couch and fell from there to the carpeted floor, Lord Montrain on his back with Maud held tightly in his arms. For a moment she gazed down into his brown eyes, feeling her body pressed intimately to the entire length of his.

Suddenly he rolled over so he was above her, and his lips trailed fiery kisses along her throat. He kissed her closed eyelids. His teeth nipped the lobes of her ears, his lips at last finding and capturing hers. Shyly at first, then with increasing ardor, finally with a passion matching his, she responded to his kiss.

As the kiss deepened, she felt as though she'd been caught and lifted by a great wave. At first she struggled against the overwhelming force but to no avail, so she let the wave carry her, lifting her higher and higher as she was swept shoreward, divided between exultation and fear, joyfully letting herself become a part of the wave even as she wondered whether it would carry her to the safety of a sheltered cove or dash her against a rocky shore.

His lips left hers. She opened her eyes, looked up at his face hovering above her only a breath away. Again he kissed her, quickly this time, again he gazed down at her, his brown eyes suddenly soft with tenderness.

What did he read in her eyes? she wondered. That she was his and his alone? Suddenly afraid, she used all the willpower she possessed to struggle back from the brink of complete surrender. It would never do to have him realize how helpless she was where he was concerned.

Why couldn't she be coy and flirtatious, why couldn't she behave as though they had world enough, and time? Only moments before he'd berated her, almost reducing her to tears, and now with a few kisses he meant to make her forget the reason she'd come to Blackstone House. *Had* made her forget for long moments.

"Gwen," she managed to say.

Lord Montrain scowled. He tried to kiss her again, but she forced herself to turn her head away. "It's a long and complicated story," he said.

"Tell me."

He curled one of her ringlets around his forefinger. "My lovely inquisitive Maud," he murmured. His fingers left her hair to tingle a path across her cheek and then touch her lips.

What did Gwen's visit here matter? Or the fact that Mrs. Wilcomb would return from the next room at any moment? She looked up at him again, and this time her lips sought his.

There was a sharp rapping.

She gasped and looked toward the hall door. Lord Montrain, muttering an oath, sprang to his feet, reached down, and helped her rise. Sitting on the settee, she hurriedly smoothed her rumpled skirt.

The door opened and Philip Faurot stepped into the room. "I hope I'm not intruding," he said with an ironical bow to Maud.

Lord Montrain straightened his coat; Maud's hand went to her tousled hair. "Not at all," Lord Montrain told him. "Lady Maud and I were discussing—" He paused, frowning. "We were discussing

165

the Ashton Fair," he improvised.

"M. Lusignon intends to give a fencing exhibition," she added.

Philip crossed the room to them, pausing to pick up her bonnet from the floor. "During your discussion of the Ashton Fair, you seem to have dropped this," he said, handing the hat to her.

Maud's face flamed as she accepted her bonnet and put it on.

"So Maurice Lusignon intends to display his fencing skill," Philip said. "That's an opportunity I find difficult to ignore."

"Dash it all, Philip," Lord Montrain said, "with pistols you'd stand a chance against Lusignon but not with rapiers. He's a master."

"Affairs of honor appeal to me." Philip looked directly at Lord Montrain. "I've been reading one of your English poets, Lovelace, who has something to say on the subject. These lines have a certain ring to them, don't you agree, John? Listen. 'I could not love thee, dear, so much, Loved I not honor more.' "

"*Touché,*" Lord Montrain said.

Did he sound chastened? Maud wondered. She realized there was a hidden meaning to Philip Faurot's words, but she couldn't fathom precisely what it was. Aware the American didn't want her here, she was pondering how to say her goodbyes gracefully when Philip looked down at the chessboard and then glanced at her.

Frowning, he took an ornate gold snuffbox from his pocket, idly shifting it from hand to hand while staring at the board. As he studied the chess pieces,

166

Maud studied him. Could he be the heartless Guy Gournay described to her by M. Lusignon? Would women be drawn to him? He was shorter and darker than Lord Montrain, his eyes a piercing blue. She supposed some women might find him handsome, and in different circumstances perhaps he could be charming. She certainly hadn't found him so.

Finally Philip looked up from the board and smiled. "A clever ploy with the bishop, Lady Maud," he admitted, "yet futile." He moved his rook. "I think you'll have to admit it's mate in three moves."

She thought through the possible moves, then nodded. Her position *was* rendered hopeless by Philip Faurot's strategy. "Perhaps Lord Montrain can devise a better play for white," she said.

Philip smiled sardonically. "That's hardly likely." He opened his snuffbox, took a pinch and inhaled, took another and inhaled again. "John doesn't play the game."

So it was Philip Faurot who played chess, not Lord Montrain! Did that mean he was the one who'd sparked Gwen's interest in learning the game? Gwen and Philip? Possibly, though it seemed an unlikely pairing to her.

The connecting door opened and Mrs. Wilcomb came into the room, leaning on her cane as she glanced from Maud to the two gentlemen. Maud hastened to introduce them.

"I hope you and Lord Montrain had time for a pleasant chat," she said to Maud.

Before she could reply, Philip, his lips curled

in a sly smile, answered for her. "I'm given to understand they discussed the Ashton Fair."

Maud glared at him. He not only lacked charm, but he was rude. A boor.

"What an unusual snuffbox," Mrs. Wilcomb said to Philip. "The elder Mr. Plimsall collects them. I'm certain he'd be interested in adding one like it to his collection."

Philip looked down at the gold box in his hand before slipping it into his pocket. "If so," he said, "I fear he'll have to suffer a disappointment. This is one of a kind, a gift to me from my father on my eighteenth birthday."

Snuffboxes, Maud thought, she wasn't in the least interested in snuffboxes. Now she *would* say their goodbyes.

When Lord Montrain bowed over her hand, he gazed intently into her eyes, almost pleadingly she thought, but he said nothing. Only a short time before she'd been convinced he intended to explain himself, but Philip Faurot's appearance had dashed that hope. Though her heart pounded disobediently, she somehow managed to appear cool and aloof while Montrain escorted them from the house and handed them into the phaeton. As she urged the horse away from Blackstone House, she refused to look back.

Driving along the London road, Maud, still shaken by Lord Montrain's passionate kisses and still confused by his refusal to be candid, tried to collect her thoughts. He must love her, she assured herself. She couldn't bear to think that her heart would betray her in this way if he didn't. And since

168

it was Philip Faurot who played chess, Gwen might have ridden to Blackstone House to see him, not Lord Montrain. Though why Gwen would prefer Mr. Faurot to Lord Montrain was an enigma.

"Does that gentleman have another name?" Mrs. Wilcomb asked.

Surprised, Maud glanced sideways at her companion. "Another name? Do you mean Lord Montrain? It's John Severn, but I thought you knew that."

"Of course I do. I mean his friend, Mr. Philip Faurot."

"Not that I'm aware of. Why do you ask?"

"Because the initial I saw inscribed on Mr. Philip Faurot's snuffbox was neither a *P* nor an *F*. It was most decidedly a *G*."

Chapter Twelve

With one hand clutching the paisley shawl covering her head and shoulders, Maud started down Montague Street in the littered warren of streets that was Spitalfields. The pungent odor from a nearby brewery mingling with the stench of ordure and other filth brought the taste of bile to her mouth, but she forced herself to walk on. Her purpose was too important to be impeded by niceties.

Through a broken window she heard the cackling laugh of a drunken crone. When a man called an indelicate invitation to her from across the street, she recoiled but after a brief hesitation hurried on, afraid yet determined, pulling the concealing shawl closer as she counted the dilapidated houses to her right.

Coming to the ninth building, she stopped, then climbed the steps to the door and knocked. There was no answer, so she turned the knob, pushed the door open, and entered, finding herself in a hallway with plastered walls that were cracked and stained.

A stairway rose into darkness a short distance ahead of her; she saw a closed door to her right and another to her left. Opening the right-hand door, she stepped inside a shadowed room smelling of must and decay. Broken panes in the windows had been stuffed with papers and cloths. As her eyes grew accustomed to the darkness, she made out the form of a woman lying on a pile of straw in front of a cold hearth.

"Gwen?" she said.

The woman moaned. Was it possible she'd responded by saying "Maud"? Had she found her sister at last?

Crossing the room and kneeling at the woman's side, Maud stared down at a gaunt yet familiar face. "Gwen," she cried, "it *is* you." Tears of joy filled her eyes. "I'm here to take you home to Twin Oaks," she told her sister.

"Dear Maud." Gwen's voice was no more than a hoarse whisper. "Thank God you've come." Gwen coughed when she tried to speak, then coughed again and again, the dry painful paroxysms racking her wasted body.

Maud hardly recognized this woman as the vibrant Gwen she'd last seen a little more than a year ago at Twin Oaks. Impulsively she leaned down and hugged her sister, kissing her hot, flushed cheek.

"Papa?" Gwen asked. "Can he ever bring himself to forgive me?"

"These last months he's been like a man possessed, a man who should be in Bedlam. Forgive you? He forgave you long ago, dear Gwen, and since that day he's searched high and low for you. Now his only desire is to have you return home where we can take care of you. Where we can make you well again."

"I only pray to God you've not come too late."

171

Silently, Maud echoed her sister's prayer.

With Maud's help, Gwen struggled to her feet. Her gown was soiled and torn, her once lustrous dark hair fell dull and limp around her shoulders. As she shuffled to the inglenook, Maud, looking beyond her, for the first time noticed a cradle.

When Gwen leaned over the cradle, Maud gently stopped her by putting a hand on her arm and bending down to pick up the swaddled baby. The infant started crying fitfully, so Maud held him to her shoulder and patted his back while murmuring soothing words of comfort. After a few minutes his crying stopped.

"I had him christened Percival Gournay," Gwen said. "Papa's first name." Her voice caught as she added, "And Guy's last."

Trying to think of words that might serve to comfort her sister, Maud said, "Papa is having the box room in the west wing made over into a nursery."

Gwen didn't seem to hear. "I'll be scorned and shunned," she lamented. "Never again will I be able to hold up my head in society. What a fool I was to believe Guy when he told me he was a wealthy émigré able to return to France now that the Bourbons have been restored to the throne, that he had to use an alias and meet me secretly because his life was threatened by the villainous M. Lusignon, that he and Lord Montrain would go to France and he'd return forthwith to England to marry me. To think that I believed him without question." Gwen began to sob softly.

Was it Guy's supposed wealth that had attracted Gwen? Maud wondered, recalling that her sister always seemed to favor suitors who were plump in the pocket. She shook her head, warning herself not to be mean-spirited in her thoughts of her sister, especially not now. "Men are masterful deceivers," she replied.

"I recall that Papa tried to warn me, but to my sorrow I failed to heed him." Gwen paused. "Has there been any word of Guy? Any word at all?"

Hearing the lilt of hope in her voice, Maud realized, with a shock of surprise, that her sister still harbored feelings of tenderness for her betrayer. How could she after all she'd been through, the months of lonely wandering, the degradation? And yet didn't she, Maud, often suppress a wistful longing for Lord Montrain despite his duplicity, imagining he'd someday return for her?

"There's been no word of either of them," Maud said. "Last week I rode to Blackstone House and found it deserted and falling into ruin. Papa believes those two scoundrels have traveled to France but not to reclaim Guy's estates, they were mere ploys in his scheme of seduction, but to escape the revenge of the London moneylenders, the cent-per-centers."

"How fortunate you were, Maud, to avoid my sad fate."

"I must confess that my mistrust of Philip Faurot (I still think of him by that name rather than Guy Gournay) and Lord Montrain came about because of the timely warnings of my dear friend, M. Maurice Lusignon."

"How I misjudged that gentleman, thinking him an evil servant of Satan when in fact he had only our best interests at heart from the day he arrived at Twin Oaks. If I, too, had listened to M. Lusignon I wouldn't be where you find me now."

Holding little Percival Gournay close, Maud put her other arm around Gwen, who, before allowing herself to be helped to the door, donned a once-modish bonnet adorned with drooping and faded pink roses.

"Dear Gwen," Maud said, "the future won't be as bleak as you might imagine. After our return home to Twin Oaks and to Papa, you and I will care for dear Percival, making certain to instill in him the Christian virtues of truth, honor, and constancy. I intend to join the Society for Encouraging the Safe Return of Girls to Their Homes in the Country. We'll spend our lives doing good works and never, never marry."

And so the Hawthorn sisters, Maud and Gwen, with their heads high and at least a modicum of hope in their hearts, ventured out into the teeming streets of Spitalfields to begin their new life. Together . . .

Opening her eyes, Maud looked about her at the red roses climbing the sides and spilling over the top of the arbor. After dabbing a leftover tear from her eye, she drew in a deep breath of the cool morning air as she sought to escape the spell of her daydream.

How foolish her imaginings sometimes were, she told herself, how absurd to foresee such calamities befalling Gwen merely because of an initial on a snuffbox. Lord Montrain would never be a party to such a hoax, for Lord Montrain was a true and honorable man. He was, wasn't he? Yes, she assured herself. If he were helping Philip Faurot conceal his identity, he must have a good and sufficient reason beyond the bonds of friendship.

She would, however, make Gwen aware of her suspicions at the first opportunity. If her sister was being deceived in any way by the American, it was her bounden duty to warn her.

Rising from the bench, Maud brushed off the skirts of her green riding habit. Now she must find Tom: she'd put off that unpleasant task long enough. Old Cob would be expecting them in the east meadow within the hour.

To own the truth, she was hesitant to ask a favor of Tom. Though she'd known the groom almost all of her life, they had never been easy with one another, probably, she suspected, because from the day she'd received her first pony she'd gone to Old Cob for advice about horses and riding. Tom had resented the old gypsy.

Her father and Tom, on the other hand, were more like friends than master and servant since they shared an interest in hunting foxes and shooting game. The two men could spend hours debating the relative merits of a hound, a horse, or a favorite firearm.

Her relations with Tom, she thought with a slight smile, were not dissimilar to the dealings of England with France except they never erupted into open warfare. She was the Duke of Wellington; he was Napoleon. When the duke had faced Napoleon on the battlefield at Waterloo two years before, she reminded herself, he had done so with élan. She intended to be equally bold with Tom.

Maud marched to the stables with a show of more confidence than she felt. She discovered Tom in the yard, a brush in his hand and a bucket at his feet, washing the traveling chaise. She advanced resolutely until she was a few feet from him.

Tom turned to her, touching his cap with his free hand. Short and red-haired, the middle-aged head groom had a foxlike face and a quick, irritable manner.

Without preliminaries, Maud launched her attack. "If you'll saddle Ne'er-Do-Well and Juno," she told him, "we can ride to the east meadow where I'd like you to put Ne'er-Do-Well through his paces."

Tom, holding his ground, dropped the brush into the pail and crossed his arms. "I'm right sorry, my lady," he said, without sounding in the least bit sorry, "but his lordship wants this here chaise washed by noontime. Told me so yesterday."

"I asked my father," Maud said quietly yet firmly, "if you could help me with Ne'er-Do-Well, and he agreed." On Saturday evening while her father had been busy with his computations, she'd mentioned having Tom assist her. "Yes, yes, of course," Lord Ashley had said.

"That ain't what I was given to understand." After thus repelling her initial thrust, Tom mounted a counterattack. "If you was to talk to his lordship again, my lady, you'd see I'm right when I says he wants the chaise washed good and proper. And wants it done this very morning."

Before leaving the house, Maud's brief reconnaissance had discovered that her father had left Twin Oaks shortly after breakfast to ride to Ashton to call on his solicitor. Since Tom was certainly aware of this, his suggestion was at least insincere and at most defiant.

Annoyed, she said, "My father's in Ashton, so I can't very well ask him."

"Now I recollect he did say something about riding into the village." Tom made a show of looking around the empty yard. "As you can see, my lady," he told her, "there's no one here to wash the chaise. 'Cepting me. My riding Ne'er-Do-Well has to wait for another day, seems to me."

Touching his cap to her, he turned and began scrubbing the side of the carriage while at the same time whistling a Scottish air. Her face flamed. She opened her mouth to argue with him, decided to hold her tongue, and started to walk angrily away only to shake her head and stop. No, she wouldn't retreat, she wouldn't let Mr. Tom Whittaker defeat her. If she gave in now, she'd never be able to stand up to him again.

"Tom," she said quietly yet firmly.

He either didn't hear her or pretended not to, for he kept whistling.

"Tom!" she repeated, louder this time.

He stopped scrubbing the carriage door and turned to face her with the brush in one hand and the bucket in the other. "Ma'am?" he said.

"Tom," she told him, "I've asked Old Cob to meet us in the east meadow at ten this morning."

When he started to protest, she silenced him with a quick shake of her head. "I want you to saddle

177

Ne'er-Do-Well and Juno at once and bring both horses to the main entrance. If my father says anything to you about the chaise not being washed, you're to tell him you were following my orders. Do you understand?"

Tom stared at her, his mouth agape.

"Do you understand?" Maud asked again. Though her voice sounded resolute enough in her ears, in reality she was all aflutter, fearing the groom would defy her and not knowing how she'd respond if he did.

Tom put the bucket on the ground and dropped the brush in the soapy water. He removed his cap and for a moment he glared at her. "Yes, my lady," he said at last, "I'll have the horses in the front afore you know it."

"Thank you, Tom," she said.

Walking back to the house, she felt a warm sense of satisfaction, of accomplishment. Hers had been a small victory, perhaps, no more than the saddling of two horses, and yet small victories sowed the seeds of great ones, and thus wars were won.

And girls became women.

The day had started badly for Lord Ashley. His solicitor, Mr. Herbert Trivel, had agreed that his lordship's financial situation demanded immediate action of the most unpleasant sort, namely the sale of a considerable portion of the Twin Oaks estate. Mr. Trivel proposed entering into negotiations with Mr. Robert Plimsall at the soonest possible moment since Mr. Plimsall had expressed an interest in increasing his holdings.

Lord Ashley, feeling the spur of necessity and unwilling to have his estate encumbered, reluctantly agreed.

Upon his return to Twin Oaks following this humiliating interview, Lord Ashley was at once confronted with the sight of his traveling chaise, partially clean and partially streaked with dust and dirt, sitting unattended in the stable yard. He had told Tom to have the chaise scrubbed inside and out by noon, and since it was now lacking but five minutes of that hour, his order had obviously been regarded lightly.

By the time he found young Harry washing out the kennels, Lord Ashley's foot had begun to throb. Earlier that morning, the boy informed him, Tom had ridden off to parts unknown accompanied by Lady Maud. The groom had left perhaps an hour ago, Harry said, leaving the time of his return uncertain.

Wearied, frustrated, and angry, Lord Ashley told the lad to have Tom come to him at the very instant of his reappearance. Lord Ashley then limped to the house where he closeted himself in the smoking room with that favorite solace of the unhappy and the misunderstood, a glass of Scotch whiskey.

One by one, his lordship listed his discontents: his debts were onerous and growing more so; his daughter Gweneth seemed destined to make a habit of losing her heart to the most inappropriate of suitors; his daughter Maud was not only naive, she refused to listen to the advice of those more experienced than she—meaning himself; and in direct proportion to the increase of his troubles, his gout worsened.

Now that he had listed his discontents, he proceeded to examine them one by one. Why, he had been asked, didn't he decrease the size of his wagers? He smiled at such a question. To wager merely a pound or two on the deal of the cards or the fall of the dice or the speed and stamina of a thoroughbred was, to Lord Ashley, not to wager at all since a small bet failed to stir in him the hope of winning or the fear of losing.

As for his daughters, he neither understood them nor held out much hope of ever understanding or influencing them. If only his wife had lived!

Which left his final source of discontent, the bane of the gout. Dr. Stephens had prescribed cold baths and a diet of broths, puddings, and jellies for his physical affliction. And declaimed at some length and with considerable force on the merits of abstinence. The cure was worse than the disease, by God.

In addition to these miseries, he was lonely.

Lord Ashley put down his glass and sat up straight in his armchair. Lonely? What had prompted him to add loneliness to the list of his afflictions? How could he be lonely? Didn't he have his London clubs, his hunting, his shooting and fishing, his games of whist, his dinners, his friends and his family? And yet, on reflection, he couldn't deny there was something missing from his life.

Frowning, he started to turn the matter over in his mind when there was a rapping at the smoking-room door. In answer to Lord Ashley's summons,

Tom entered and stood holding his cap deferentially in both hands in front of him.

"I saw the chaise in the stable yard," Lord Ashley said with a hard look in his eyes.

"I'll have her clean in an hour's time," Tom told him.

"That will be two hours past noon." Lord Ashley, usually not a stickler, wasn't about to let the matter drop easily. Not today.

"Lady Maud asked me to bring Ne'er-Do-Well to the east meadow to give him a run. She said you'd agreed, milord."

So Maud was behind this. *Had* she asked his leave? For the life of him, Lord Ashley couldn't recall. As usual, Tom had reasons and explanations for everything he'd done which explained why Lord Ashley usually avoided discussions such as this. Looking at Tom, he saw by the eager expression on his face that the groom had more to tell.

"Out with it, man," he said. "I can see you're fit to burst."

" 'Tis Ne'er-Do-Well. We ran him a mile and a half, like in a race, and I held him in check till the last two furlongs and then I let him go, spurring him a bit, and he closed with a mighty rush that fair took me breath away. We didn't have a clock on him, but I swear Vulcan would've had his hands full if he'd faced him today."

"And this was Maud's doing?"

Tom frowned. "I'm a man who gives the devil his due. Old Cob put her up to it."

"Old Cob!" Lord Ashley's face turned a deeper red. "That damn gypsy was there with you?"

"Looking spry despite his years."

Tom went on to describe Ne'er-Do-Well's surprising performance in some detail, but Lord Ashley didn't hear him. He'd told Maud that Old Cob wasn't to set foot on Twin Oaks soil, he remembered the conversation distinctly, and she'd seen fit to defy him. Maud, too audacious for her own good, needed a proper set down.

Reining in his anger—Maud's flouting of his authority was no concern of Tom's—he waited for a pause in the groom's narrative and quickly thanked and dismissed him. He was surprised when Tom hesitated instead of leaving the room at once.

"There was one thing more I might be mentioning," Tom said.

Good God, what now? Bracing himself for the worst, Lord Ashley nodded for Tom to go on.

" 'Twas when I was washing the chaise like you told me." Tom paused as though to be certain his employer appreciated his devotion to duty. "Lady Maud said to saddle the two horses and I was saying no without saying the words, if you follow me, and she stood up to me and said, 'Saddle the horses,' like she'd been mistress of Twin Oaks for years instead of being the young lass she is."

Lord Ashley scowled. First she'd defied him over Old Cob, and now she thought of herself as mistress of Twin Oaks!

"Begging your pardon if I'm over the line," Tom said with a slight smile, "but, just between you, me, and the gatepost, Lady Maud called to mind somebody else putting me in my place years ago."

"Are you referring to her mother?" Lord Ashley

was puzzled because his wife had always been loath to give orders to the outside help.

"No, it's yourself I mean. I was thinking of the hound."

Remembering, Lord Ashley nodded. Shortly after Tom had been hired at Twin Oaks, Lord Ashley, objecting to the groom's handling of one of the hounds, had set him straight in short order. Tom had actually seemed relieved at the reprimand, his respect for Lord Ashley had increased tenfold, and they were soon friends.

"If there's nothing more," Tom said, "I'll get on with the cleaning of the chaise."

He waved his hand in dismissal. After Tom had gone, he pondered what he'd heard. At any other time learning that Maud took after him would have pleased Lord Ashley but not today. Today her flouting his prohibition of Old Cob overrode all else, and what he would normally have seen as a sign of maturity he viewed as a fatal tendency on the part of his younger daughter to rise above her station. She wasn't mistress of Twin Oaks, by God.

About to summon his errant daughter, he was surprised by a tapping at the door. Thinking Tom had returned, he called to him to enter. When the door opened, Maud burst into the room, her face aglow with excitement.

"Oh, Papa," she cried, "Ne'er-Do-Well should be held back so he can make his run at the finish. Tom rode him in the east meadow this morning and the horse did ever so well. It's because his bloodline goes back to Eclipse."

"Pray sit, Maud," Lord Ashley told her coldly.

"Tom has already informed me of your little excursion to the meadow."

Maud perched on the edge of a chair. "You will race him in the Canterbury Stakes at Newmarket, won't you, Papa? He has every chance of winning, and the odds should be at least twenty to one against him."

What a sly minx she was to appeal to his sporting instincts, he thought, even as her enthusiasm roused his own. The Canterbury Stakes indeed; the horse didn't stand a chance whether racing from in front or from behind. Her mention of the Stakes, though, solved the question of how to punish her for disobeying him. He'd refuse to race Ne'er-Do-Well.

"It was all Old Cob's doing," said Maud. "He knew of Ne'er-Do-Well's ancestry. He suggested the change."

"Ah, so Old Cob was with you at the meadow." He was surprised to hear her own the truth.

"Papa, I remembered your saying Old Cob couldn't set foot on Twin Oaks land, so Tom and I arrived at the meadow early so I could intercept him. I made certain he sat on the knoll on the edge of Plimsall land to watch Tom ride Ne'er-Do-Well. He never crossed the Twin Oaks boundary, and I'll see to it he never will for as long as you forbid him."

Lord Ashley stared at his daughter in amazement. How he'd wronged her! It was as plain as a pikestaff that she'd obeyed him in every particular. Now he saw her treatment of Tom in its true light, not as presumption but as befitting her position in life.

184

His guilt mingled with his desperate need for money as he attempted to determine a way to reward her. The answer sprang easily to mind.

"Ne'er-Do-Well will race in the Canterbury Stakes," he promised.

Maud threw her arms around his neck and kissed him. "You're the best father in all the world," she told him.

After a jubilant Maud left to tell Gwen that they would be traveling to Newmarket, Lord Ashley leaned back in his chair and closed his eyes. There was hope for Maud, after all, he thought, and perhaps Gwen would surprise him as well. Did Ne'er-Do-Well have a chance of winning the Stakes? Probably not, but still he couldn't help but picture numbers chalked on a board: 20-I, 25-1, 30-1. In his mind's eye he saw Ne'er-Do-Well surge from the pack and gallop into the lead.

It was at this moment that Lord Ashley experienced a strange feeling, an enveloping warmth that he was able, after considerable thought, to identify as contentment. Even the pain in his foot was gone.

Now all I need to be perfectly happy, he told himself, is a wife.

Chapter Thirteen

Maud was determined to warn her sister of the likelihood that Mr. Philip Faurot, aided and abetted by Lord Montrain, was not only concealing his true identity but was doing so with a dishonorable intent. Although her overriding desire was to save Gwen from possible harm, she also wanted to lighten the burden of her knowledge of the deception by sharing it.

Each time Maud approached her sister, however, Gwen seemed to use various stratagems to avoid an intimate discussion. The probable reason, Maud surmised, was that her sister suspected the nature of the proposed tête-à-tête. No woman welcomed being told she was making a mistake in an affair of heart; such advice was particularly distasteful coming from a younger sister.

A few days before their departure for Newmarket, Maud, undaunted by Gwen's rebuffs, confronted her sister after dinner and suggested a stroll. When Gwen frowned and put her hand to her forehead, Maud wondered if she intended to plead a case of the dismals but then, with a sigh of resignation, Gwen nodded her agreement.

They followed a path winding among the shrubbery, each silent and preoccupied with her own thoughts. Maud spoke first. "When *I* suffered from the megrims," she said, "my—" She had been about to say "dear friend," but her feeling of closeness to M. Lusignon had faded with the passing of time since their conversation in the garden. She went on in a more formal vein. "M. Lusignon," she said, "was able to effect a cure in a matter of minutes with the aid of his pocket watch."

"His watch? Don't be a goose, Maud. I've never heard of a watch curing anything except a case of habitual tardiness."

"Nor had I before I met M. Lusignon." Maud described how the Frenchman had used the techniques of a physician named Mesmer to relieve her headache.

"I certainly wouldn't submit to any such treatment at the hands of M. Lusignon," Gwen said with more than a touch of asperity. "I've not liked him from the first, and why you, Maud, saw fit to put such trust in him I don't understand."

If M. Lusignon was able to cure her headache, Maud mused, by using his powers of persuasion while she was in a trance, what else might he be able to do? What other suggestions might he place in her mind without her being aware of them? In the future, she decided, she'd best be on her guard against M. Lusignon's mesmerism.

She still felt called upon to defend him to her sister. "If you'll recall Elizabeth Bennet's initial prejudice against Mr. Darcy because of his pride," she said, "you'll realize that our first impressions are notoriously poor guides to a man's character.

M. Lusignon has our best interests at heart; he's been honest with us which is more than I can say for certain other gentlemen of our acquaintance."

"I expect you refer to Mr. Faurot and Lord Montrain."

"None other." She told Gwen about Mrs. Wilcomb seeing the letter *G* engraved on Philip Faurot's snuffbox.

"I daresay you've observed how low Mrs. Wilcomb bends over her embroidery," said Gwen, "and so you realize how very nearsighted she is even when wearing her spectacles. And yet you accuse Mr. Faurot of deceit based on no more than Mrs. Wilcomb's interpretation of an initial on a snuffbox. She's undoubtedly muddled on the point. It's not like you to be so unfair, Maud."

There was no doubt that Mrs. Wilcomb's eyesight was poor. Could I, Maud wondered, have been too ready to suspect that Philip Faurot was living a lie?

"I have other reasons to believe Mr. Faurot isn't who he claims to be," Maud said in her own defense. When her sister began to question her, she held up her hand and went on. "Though I'm not at liberty to reveal the name of my informant."

"It can only be M. Lusignon." Gwen took Maud's hand and squeezed it affectionately. "Don't trust him, Maud. Don't be taken in by his Parisian charm."

"Who *can* I trust?" Maud asked. Not Gwen, she thought, not Philip Faurot, perhaps not even Lord Montrain.

Gwen started to answer, then abruptly stopped herself. Her sister, Maud observed, was behaving much as Lord Montrain had at Blackstone House, as though she wanted to speak yet felt compelled for reasons unknown to remain silent.

Gwen released Maud's hand. "Now I am feeling a bit weary," she said, "so I believe I'll go to my chamber and rest." Without another word she turned and hurried back to the house, leaving Maud staring after her. Maud could never remember feeling so abandoned. So alone.

The days passed slowly for Maud, but at last she, her sister, her father, and the stable chicken, Little, were on their way to Newmarket in the chaise.

Maud had neither heard from nor seen Lord Montrain since the Sunday she'd visited Blackstone House. To keep her thoughts from fruitless speculation regarding his behavior, she tried to start a conversation, wondering whether the hot dry weather would have an influence on the condition of the turf and hence on the outcome of the race, but her companions answered in monosyllables or not at all, so she soon abandoned the effort.

She couldn't help wondering whether her father was concealing a change for the worse in the state of his health. Lately she'd noticed he often sat in the smoking room without his customary glass of whiskey and at the dinner table seemed to have developed a remarkable appetite for broths, puddings, and jellies. Worried, she made up her mind to ask him before they returned home from Newmarket.

Their journey was uneventful until shortly after they left the stones north of Islington on the outskirts of London.

"Gwen, Papa," Maud said, "see how the people along the way are pointing and gazing skyward."

Her father, who had been dozing fitfully, looked out of the window. "Strange," he said. He rapped on the roof, and after the chaise came to a halt, stepped down to the heat-baked dirt of the road. "You must both alight," he told them, "for I'll warrant you've never witnessed such a sight before."

When Maud and Gwen joined him, they looked up and saw, far above the rooftops and the chimneys, a white balloon rising into the pale blue sky. One of the passengers in the basket suspended below the balloon's envelope leaned over the side and waved a flag. The spectators on the ground hurrahed.

"The balloon is filled with gas, perhaps hydrogen," Lord Ashley explained, "and since the gas is lighter than air, the balloon rises. By releasing the gas, the pilot allows the balloon to descend."

Filled with awe, they watched the balloon until it was out of sight. Once they were on their way again, Lord Ashley said, "You'll both live to see great changes in our world, men flying from city to city in balloons, carriages like this one powered by steam huffing along the roads, ships sailing without the aid of sails."

"Aren't carriages with steam engines usually run on rails?" Maud asked.

"In the mines, yes, and for the purpose of exhibition to the public. But when steam becomes common, rails won't be used. I say this for two reasons. First, the laying of iron rails is expensive and, second, with rails you must travel where the rails lead, not where you want to go."

Maud nodded. What her father said made eminent sense.

"I try to keep myself well-informed regarding scientific matters," Lord Ashley said, "and I've always insisted that you and Gwen receive a general education. Not only have I made certain you learned womanly skills such as knitting, painting, dancing, and music, but I've also had you instructed in science, history, and geography."

"Mrs. Wilcomb always demanded that we read books on a wide variety of subjects," Gwen said.

"I attempted to initiate a conversation with a young lady at the Plimsalls' ball." Lord Ashley shook his head in exasperation. "She seemed to have the notion that the French Revolution took place several centuries ago rather than during my own youth."

"The Bastille was stormed on July 14, 1789," Gwen intoned as though repeating the words from memory.

"The mistake men make when they decide to marry at a mature age such as mine," Lord Ashley went on, "is in seeking the same qualities they admired when they were young rather than seeking out an older woman who's unaffected and accomplished. The reason, I expect, is that while the flesh grows old, the mind does not. We imagine ourselves younger than we actually are."

Maud looked quizzically at her father. Marriage? Could Gwen have been right in suspecting their father was considering marriage?

"I, for one," Lord Ashley said, "find it most difficult to converse intelligently with young women."

"You converse with us," Maud pointed out.

"As we've just established, you both have the advantage· of a diverse education. However, as men and women grow older, particularly if they're well attuned to one another, they tend to converse not only with their words but with their silences. While we three converse well in words, we don't in our silences."

"Papa," Maud exclaimed, "I believe you're funning us. Converse in silences, indeed!"

"I swear it's true. Have you never heard of a speaking look? Words aren't needed when you're able to use the tilt of the head, the arch of an eyebrow, or a particular smile to convey your message."

"What I find appealing in a gentleman," Gwen said, "is not so much his silences, no matter how interesting or profound they may be, but a certain wit, a certain worldly consequence, a certain income, and, of course, an ability to arouse a feeling of tenderness."

Maud frowned. "To my mind, love is all that matters."

She would only marry for love, Maud assured herself, and since she could only love one man and that one man seemed to change direction with every change in the weather, probably she wouldn't marry at all.

"A youthfully romantic but dangerous sentiment, my dear Maud," said her father. "The young would do well to emulate some of the Oriental civilizations

192

where the parents of the young man or the young woman, with the benefit of their love for their children and their greater experience, arrange the marriage without consulting the child. This is much superior to the English arrangement where the father has only the power of a veto."

"Do you want me to believe," Gwen asked, "that you could make a better choice of a husband for me than I could for myself? Or Maud could for herself?"

"I'm confident I could."

Maud suppressed a smile since, where Gwen was concerned, she couldn't help agreeing with her father. But if he tried to choose for me, she told herself, the result would be nothing less than disastrous.

"If you were considering marriage for yourself, Papa," Maud said, "and if dear Grandpapa and Grandmama were still alive, that would mean you should defer the choice of your bride to them."

"Not at all. It's a well-known fact that a man reaches the height of his reasoning powers in the fourth decade of his life, after which a gradual decline commences. It follows that at my age I would be best qualified to choose for myself as well as for you and Gwen."

"The result of an arrangement such as you describe," Gwen said, "would be domestic disharmony with bride and groom continually at odds."

Lord Ashley shook his head. "Do you maintain that at present we English are blessed with domestic peace? Isn't it a truism that, after the excitement of their courtship and their subsequent union, husbands and wives more often than not go their separate ways?"

"You and Mama didn't," Maud pointed out.

"If I placed a china cup on the ground," Lord Ashley said, "and threw a stone at it from a distance of twenty paces and happened to hit it, would that prove that the best way to break pieces of china was to throw stones at them from a distance? Of course not."

"We weren't talking of stone throwing," Maud said, "but of marriage, which, I hope you'll agree, are usually quite different. You must admit that very few of our English marriages end in divorce."

"Because the barriers to divorce are so unscalable," Lord Ashley said. "I'm given to understand that in certain Middle Eastern countries a woman divorces her husband merely by placing his shoes on the doorstep of their house. If England adopted such a custom, shoemakers would become wealthy from having to replace the great number of shoes left outside to be stolen or ruined by inclement weather."

"If I should happen to marry, though I doubt I ever will," Maud said as her thoughts returned, unbid, to Lord Montrain, "I'd expect the match to last forever."

"As would I," Gwen echoed.

"In the course of my life," Lord Ashley said, "I've observed this difference between men and women. Men argue from general principles to reach valid, far-reaching conclusions while women always insist on applying those principles only to themselves."

"I don't," said Maud.

194

"Nor I," said Gwen.

Lord Ashley nodded, crossed his arms, and said, "I consider my case proved." To Maud's vexation, he thereupon closed his eyes, thus precluding further discussion of the subject.

On the day of the Canterbury Stakes, Maud visited Ne'er-Do-Well's stall shortly before the horses were to be summoned for the start of the race.

"Sam Chifney's our jockey," Tom told her, "and lucky we were to get him." Tom, she noticed, had been eager to please her ever since the day she'd insisted he ride with her to the meadow. "He's known," Tom added, "for his sure judgment of the pace but 'specially his strong finishes, so much so they're called the 'Chifney Rush.' "

"Even so, my father says Ne'er-Do-Well's listed as twenty-five to one against." Maud was distressed because her father had wagered heavily on their horse. She blamed herself at least in part; she shouldn't have been so enthusiastic about his chances.

When the call came for the horses to proceed to the paddock, Tom led Ne'er-Do-Well out of his stall. Maud started to follow when she came face-to-face with Lord Montrain.

Staring, she drew in her breath. For days she'd pictured herself meeting him here at Newmarket at one of the balls or while strolling in the city or at the racecourse itself or later at the Jockey Club dinner, yet despite all her imaginings she was totally unprepared for the actuality.

This puzzled her, for he looked much as she'd thought he would, carrying a gold-knobbed walking stick and dressed in top hat, light blue coat, dark blue trousers, and a checked waistcoat. She hadn't exaggerated his height in her daydreams: he was every inch as tall as she'd imagined, his hair just as dark and curling, his brown eyes as deep-set and vaguely forbidding.

Why, then, did meeting him disconcert her so? She'd carefully composed mental 'lists of innocuous subjects to discuss with him — the Stakes, the frightfully hot weather, the balloon they'd seen on their journey to Newmarket — yet now she found she couldn't speak. She'd intended to be aloof, pleasant though distant, yet how could she while she feared he must be able to hear the rapid beating of her heart?

His steady scrutiny unnerved her, causing her cheeks to redden with a vivid flush, even though she'd vowed that no possible conduct of his would disturb her. Belatedly, he tipped his hat and, his gaze still on her face, took her gloved hand and raised it to his lips. At least, Maud told herself, he seemed as nonplussed as she. She could hazard a hopeful guess as to the cause of the loss of his usual aplomb, but she couldn't be certain.

Her clothes, though new, could hardly be the culprit. She was wearing her new muslin gown of the palest green with both gown and bonnet enlivened with sea-green ribbons and, she'd feared from the first, overtrimmed, adorned as they were with lace and frills.

Lord Montrain, however, was looking not at the

196

gown but at her.

Was this one of those "speaking silences" her father had mentioned? If so, she found it much more confusing than any jumble of words might be.

Lord Montrain frowned; the frown deepened to become a scowl. He looked, she thought, most terribly severe. She waited for him to explain himself.

Expecting him to pay her a compliment, as he usually did in greeting her, she was surprised when he abruptly said, "I've been most unfair to you, Lady Maud."

She could only summon a weak, "Oh?" in reply.

"I'm certain you recall how first we met."

How could she ever forget? "You abducted me," she said.

"For which you had and have my most humble apologies. I don't expect you've forgotten the day I came upon you at the site of the monastery ruins."

"You pursued me on Vulcan. You were fierce, like a man possessed." Her breath grew short at the memory.

"For which behavior I'm truly sorry. I should have shown you greater respect. And then there was the afternoon when you unexpectedly called on my mother at Blackstone House and I inadvertently tumbled you onto the floor, embarrassing you. I hope you'll accept my apology for that unfortunate transgression."

She could only nod. It was as though, she told herself, he was attempting to wipe the slate clean of each of the moments she especially treasured. If these feelings of hers were unladylike, even perverse, so be it.

"So now that I've offered my apologies," he said with the relieved tone of someone who had fulfilled a duty, "will you join me in watching the race? I spoke to Lord Ashley a short time ago and he kindly gave his permission."

Maud hesitated. It was as though Lord Montrain had come to Newmarket bringing with him all the materials necessary to erect a wall between them and had immediately set about the task, completing it in a matter of minutes. Hurt and not a little puzzled, she wondered what other set downs he might have waiting for her.

Yet only moments before, when his gaze refused to stray from her face, her heart had told her something she had refused to admit to herself at the time — that his love matched hers. Could she have been so very wrong?

Taking her lack of reply for consent, he offered her his arm. She took it reluctantly, letting him lead her to the racecourse where he'd left his carriage guarded by his coachman. He handed her to the roof where they sat partially shaded by her sea-green parasol.

"M. Lusignon didn't journey north with you?" he asked.

"He had business in London. And what of Mr. Faurot?"

"Duty keeps him in Surrey."

They were silent for a time as she looked around them at the crush, so much greater here than at Guildford but with the same mingling of dukes and dregs, aristocrats and blacklegs, drawn hither by the races on the many courses, the gaming of all varieties, the barefisted boxing matches, the wrestling, the cock fights, the dinners, and the balls.

"There's no hogshead of claret to the winner today," she said.

"The one I won at Guildford's already consumed."

She raised her eyebrows, remembering how she'd imagined that particular hogshead being the initial cause of his ruination. "So soon," she said.

"When you distribute the contents to all those who helped you, the jockey, the grooms, all the servants at Blackstone House, a hogshead's soon emptied."

If he was to slide in disrepute, she decided with an inward smile, the cause would have to be other than the claret.

Neither spoke for a time, but before the silence became oppressive, he proceeded to introduce a variety of topics, discussing each at great length: the race and his hopes for Vulcan, the hot dry weather of the past few weeks, and *his* sighting of the balloon on *his* journey to Newmarket. Maud, who had expected to have her hopes and fears centered on Ne'er-Do-Well during these last minutes before the starter called "Go," found them instead, to her consternation, wholly taken up by her despair at not being able to fathom the motives and intentions of Lord Montrain.

The cry went up, "The horses have started!"

Lord Montrain raised his glasses to watch the spot where the thoroughbreds would first appear. Maud held her breath.

"Nothing yet," he reported. "Nothing. Nothing."

They waited; the great crowd was hushed. "There they are," he cried.

He offered her the glasses, but she shook her head.

"They're all in a jumble," he told her. "Le Pompom's in front, not Ne'er-Do-Well. Your horse must have had a poor start."

"Not at all. He's running with the others by design."

He lowered his glasses to look at her. "So you took my suggestion," he said. When she looked puzzled, he added, "About investigating your horse's bloodlines."

She recalled that he had mentioned something of the sort. "It really was Old Cob's idea," she said.

Again he raised his glasses. "Ne'er-Do-Well's the green?" he asked.

"Yes."

"Still in the midst of the pack," he told her. "Vulcan's the red. He's third." Hope threaded through his voice. "And running strongly."

The horses entered the final quarter-mile. She could make them out clearly. Le Pompom still led, but she could see he was tiring. Crusader and Vulcan ran next, then Ajax and Ne'er-Do-Well, the horses spread across the broad track. As was the custom, some of the mounted spectators galloped behind the thoroughbreds.

Le Pompom faded. Crusader forged to the front with Vulcan at his side. Ailema, the filly, burst from the pack, making her bid in the middle of the track, passing Le Pompom. Ajax and Ne'er-Do-Well ran fifth and sixth.

Now they were in the final furlong. Maud held her breath. She could hear Lord Montrain urging Vulcan on. Crusader was still first with Vulcan a head behind. Ailema hung, neither gaining nor losing ground on the outside. Ajax and Ne'er-Do-Well passed Le Pompom. The other horses trailed.

Sam Chifney, on Ne'er-Do-Well, went to the whip. The horse responded, edged past Ajax, and closed on the two leaders. Maud's heart pounded. Come on, come on, Ne'er-Do-Well, she urged silently, you can do it! Vulcan overtook Crusader, Ailema gamely rallied again on the far outside. Ne'er-Do-Well gained steadily, drawing even with Crusader. The finish post loomed.

As Vulcan dropped back, Crusader and Ne'er-Do-Well swept past him, straining forward, head to head. Ailema held steady in fourth. It was Crusader and Ne'er-Do-Well, first one thrusting his nose to the fore, then the other. Again Chifney went to the whip.

"Now!" Maud cried. "Now!"

Ne'er-Do-Well forged into the lead, crossing the line with a half-length lead.

"He won!" Maud dropped her parasol and hugged Lord Montrain. "He won!"

Lord Montrain started to put his arm around her only to draw back. "Vulcan was fourth," he said, dispirited.

"I had hoped Ne'er-Do-Well would win," Maud said, "but I never truly believed he would."

Lord Montrain muttered something that sounded like "My doing, actually."

How outrageous! His doing indeed!

"I must go to Papa," Maud said as she retrieved her parasol and scrambled down from the carriage roof with Lord Montrain, taken by surprise, following. "He'll be so elated." Not only would her father collect on his wagers at twenty-five to one, he'd receive the winner's purse of over a thousand guineas.

They found Lord Ashley surrounded by well-wishers. Gwen stood somewhat apart, her face aglow. How lovely her sister looked in her pale yellow cotton frock, Maud thought as she determinedly pushed through the crowd to her father, embracing him, kissing him on the cheek.

"I'll not have to sell the land," he whispered in her ear.

"Papa, I'm so happy for you. For us."

He drew her aside. "I'm a fair man," he told her. "I'll have Old Cob come to see me. I'll do right by him."

"I'll doubt he'll come; he's exceedingly stubborn."

"Then I'll go to him, show him I'm a man who can admit a mistake. Not that I was wrong about him in the first place, merely that I let my anger last too long."

Maud looked past him and saw Lord Montrain and Gwen walking away.

"A handsome couple," he said, following her gaze. "I gave Montrain permission to accompany your sister to our inn. He's escorting her to the Jockey Club dinner tonight as well."

Maud's joy at Ne'er-Do-Well's triumph turned to ashes.

"Don't look so crestfallen, Maud," Lord Ashley said. "I'll be your escort at the dinner. Gentlemen who don't know you will suspect I've taken up with a beautiful young lady less than half my age."

Maud forced herself to answer in the same spirit. "I'll converse with you of Marie Antoinette, Robespierre, and Marat. And the guillotine."

"The French Revolution? Of course, I remember now, the days of my youth. How envious the other gentlemen will be. I can hear them now. 'Old Ashley not only won the race,' they'll say, 'he's also found a young lady able to talk intelligently of the French Revolution.'"

She managed to smile at her father before turning her head away so he wouldn't see her tears.

Chapter Fourteen

A week passed, then another, and at last the long-anticipated day arrived. Church bells rang and flags unfurled in the warm breeze as the opening procession made its way through the village of Ashton to the music of drums, horns, and bagpipes. At the village green a crier on horseback read the age-old Royal Proclamation admonishing the populace "to keep the King's peace and make no fray, outcry, shrieking, or other noise."

And so began the first of the three carefree days of the Ashton Fair.

Philip Faurot, scorning the warnings of his friend Montrain, was determined to show his courage and uphold his honor by challenging M. Lusignon during the Frenchman's fencing demonstration at the Ashton Fair.

John Severn, Earl of Montrain, had tired of his friend's constant delays. What had begun as a wait of a week or two had lengthened into a stay in Surrey of more than two months. If Faurot didn't force the issue, *he* would, and sooner rather than later, probably during the course of the Ashton Fair.

Lord Ashley couldn't remember ever having been in better or more robust health, at least not since he was a young man. To think he owed it all to dining almost exclusively on broths, puddings, and jellies. He meant to reward himself for his success in keeping to this regimen while visiting the Ashton Fair.

Gwen, after long weeks of uncertainty, of sleepless nights and distracted days, had at last arrived at a fateful decision. What better time to tell him than the first day of the Ashton Fair.

Maud, hurt and angered by Lord Montrain's seeming vacillation, realized that being in a gay, laughing crush of pleasure-seekers would only serve to deepen her malaise. Pride, however, finally persuaded her to don a new pale yellow muslin gown and join her father, sister, and Mrs. Wilcomb in the carriage going from Twin Oaks to the Ashton Fair.

"We'll take a ramble around the grounds," Lord Ashley told them as he helped Mrs. Wilcomb alight and then offered the old woman his arm. Gwen and Maud followed them onto the fairgrounds, their parasols shading them from the August sun.

"Most of the county of Surrey must be deserted," Maud said, "for everyone is here in Ashton."

She saw yeomen, farmers, and shopkeepers with their ladies, she saw servants and children, the elderly and babes in arms, each and every one displaying his or her Sunday toggery. Dogs shared the spirit of the day by barking excitedly as they raced to and fro.

Maud's gaze was drawn to every tall gentleman in vain, for none of them turned out to be Lord Montrain. When she asked herself if she truly wanted to see him, she had to answer yes. If only so she could ignore him.

Distracted, trying not to appear overset, she

205

walked slowly past the main attractions, the tents arranged in a large semicircle, hardly noticing the colorful pictures and bold signs proclaiming the wonders waiting inside: "Punch and Judy Is Here," "Count Mirabeau and His Dancing Dogs Are Here," "Cato, The Trained Pig Is Here: Spells, Reads, Guesses Ages," "Willoughby, The World's Premier Rope Dancer, Is Here," "Madame Grimalda—Fortuneteller Extraordinary—Is Here," and "Salome Dances Here."

A smaller poster promised an archery tournament on the fair's final day, and still another gave notice that M. Lusignon's fencing exhibition would begin at two that very afternoon.

When they came to the last of the tents, Lord Ashley said, "I'm certain you'll want to inspect the offerings at the stalls, so, since I have some rather important business to conduct, I'll leave you here. We'll meet in an hour's time in front of the rope dancer's tent." Tipping his hat, he hurried off into the crowd.

Maud frowned, wondering what business her father could have on fair day. She didn't have time to ponder the matter, for almost at once Mrs. Wilcomb said, "I always feel obliged to buy something at a fair even if there's nothing I want."

Since Mrs. Wilcomb made this remark every year, Maud and Gwen said nothing in reply, having long ago exhausted all possible ripostes.

After a pause, Gwen said, "I must find the fairings stall. I've bought fairings every year since I was a little girl."

Her words brought the first smile of the day to Maud's lips. What Gwen said was true, she did always buy fairings. What her sister neglected to say was that she invariably took them home to Twin Oaks, carefully placed them in a bureau drawer, and never looked at them again.

They strolled among the stalls scattered within the semicircle of tents, breathing in the spicy aroma of gingerbread, the rich smell of baking apples, and the heavy tang of ale. Above the hum of talk and laughter, they heard a fiddler playing a lively Scottish air and the beat of a drum warning latecomers that the illusionist's performance was about to begin.

"There they are." After hurrying past a table displaying gilded gingerbread cut into the shapes of hobbyhorses and animals, Gwen stopped at the fairings stall. She exclaimed over the gifts and toys, examining each in turn, obviously torn by indecision.

"I'll take these ribbons," she told the stall keeper when, at last, she came to a decision. "They're quite the thing."

The red, green, and yellow ribbons were, Maud thought, quite pretty.

"And the silver-framed mirror," Gwen went on, "and this mug." The mug displayed the stern visage of the Duke of Wellington on one side and a British cavalry charge during the Battle of Waterloo on the other.

As soon as she received her fairings, Gwen turned to Mrs. Wilcomb. "This mirror," she said, "is a small token of how much I've appreciated all you've done for me over the years."

Mrs. Wilcomb took the mirror, blinking back tears.

"And these ribbons are for you, Maud," Gwen

207

said, "because I love you so much."

Maud stared at her sister in surprise. Taking the ribbons, she threw her arms around Gwen. "And I love you," she said softly.

Gwen returned her hug before drawing back in seeming embarrassment. Whether because she was unaccustomed to showing affection in public or because lately Lord Montrain had come between them, Maud couldn't be certain.

"The Waterloo mug's for Papa," Gwen said.

Maud nodded. "Where could he have gone to conduct business on fair day?" she wondered aloud.

On leaving his daughters with Mrs. Wilcomb, Lord Ashley strode behind the tents of the performers, hurried past the children's playground and the churchyard, slowing only when he came to the tree-shaded street leading to the Unicorn Tavern. Opening the tavern door, he paused for an instant to savor the delightfully masculine odors of stale beer and tobacco smoke.

Garvey, the Unicorn's proprietor, nodded to him in recognition from behind his bar. "Lord Ashley!" he cried. All eyes turned to the doorway.

"Ay, a toast to Lord Ashley," Mr. Smollett, the Plimsall estate agent, cried as he raised his tankard. The patrons joined in a hearty hip-hip-hoorah as Lord Ashley, immensely pleased, held up a deprecating hand.

This was the first time, as far as anyone could remember, that a visitor to the Unicorn had been greeted in such a resounding fashion. There were many reasons for the accolade, not the least of which was that Lord Ashley, besides being a genial man who spoke to everyone no matter how high or low his station, was considered to be honest in all his dealings. This good opinion was magnified on this particular day by the high spirits engendered by the fair and by the effect of the libations already consumed by the patrons of the Unicorn.

Lastly, and perchance even more importantly, although few residents of Ashton had traveled to Newmarket for the Canterbury Stakes, many of them had succeeded in one way or another in wagering small sums on the local horse, Ne'er-Do-Well. As a result of Ne'er-Do-Well's unexpected triumph, considerably more pounds and pence had found their way to Ashton than had departed that village. This served both to enrich the villagers while at the same time heightening their esteem for the horse's owner.

Lord Ashley strode to the bar. He had meant to visit the Unicorn to reward himself for his dietary self-discipline. Now he realized more was demanded of him. He rose to the challenge.

"A round for all," he announced to gratified murmurs of approval.

Taking his glass of whiskey in hand, he was about to drink it down when he spied Old Cob sitting alone in a far corner. He hesitated only a moment. "I offer a toast," Lord Ashley said, "to the man who showed me the path to victory." Saluting the gypsy with his glass, he said, "To Old Cob."

There followed a moment of silent surprise before a scattering of other voices were raised to second the toast. "To Old Cob," they echoed.

The old man pushed himself up to stand with

209

both hands clasped on the top of his walking stick. "Old Cob thanks ye, one and all." Turning to Lord Ashley, he said, "Thank ye, my lo—" He stopped abruptly.

For weeks afterwards the Unicorn regulars debated whether Old Cob, in violation of his long-held principles, had uttered the word *lord*. A few maintained he had, but the opinion of the majority was that he had not and, by God, never would as long as he lived. Who could foretell, a few of the others asked, what the next day, let alone the next year, might bring?

Madame Grimalda, for one, claimed that *she* had just such a foretelling ability and offered to reveal what she foresaw to anyone in exchange for eight pence, which was certainly, Maud thought, a modest sum to pay to be able to pierce the veil separating the present from the future.

Maud, her doubts leavened by hope, paid the admission and was ushered into the gypsy's tent where she found a single candle flame burning fitfully on a table in the center of the enclosure. She stood peering into the darkness beyond the flame as she breathed in a heavy, rather unpleasant scent she recognized as incense. At last she made out the shadowed form of a woman.

"I am Madame Grimalda," the woman said. "Come sit here beside me, my dear."

Maud wanted to say, "I don't know why I came to see you." She wanted to say, "I don't believe anyone can foretell the future." She felt a prickling along her arms. To own the truth, she did know

210

why she was here; she did believe, at least she wanted to believe.

As she became accustomed to the gloom in the tent, she saw that the olive-skinned gypsy wore a red silk shawl wrapped loosely around her shoulders, a golden bandanna over her black hair, and dangling gold earrings that glittered in the candlelight.

"Give me your hand," Madame Grimalda told her, "your right hand."

Maud extended her hand, palm up. The gypsy drew Maud's hand into the light and studied it. "An unusual mountain of Venus," she said without any great show of interest. Suddenly Maud felt the gypsy's fingers tremble and then close convulsively around her hand before releasing it.

"Your other hand." There was an urgency in Madame Grimalda's voice. When Maud stared at her, confused and with a growing unease, the gypsy said, "I must see your other hand. At once."

Maud held out her left hand. Madame Grimalda peered closely at the lines in her palm for the time it took Maud to take two quickened breaths, then released her hand and drew away into the darkness. The flickering candle threw the gypsy's shadow, wavering and vaguely threatening, onto the side of the tent behind her.

"I don't understand," Madame Grimalda said.

"What did you see?" By now Maud was thoroughly alarmed.

The fortuneteller closed her eyes and, humming softly to herself, rocked back and forth in her chair. Maud started to speak, but the gypsy raised a hand to silence her. Finally, after what seemed an eternity to Maud but was probably no more than a few minutes, Madame Grimalda stopped humming, leaned forward, and opened her eyes.

"It's not only what I read on your palm that frightens me," Madame Grimalda said, "but the vision I saw here." She placed her fingers on her temple. "There are two men in your life," she went on slowly as though groping her way in unfamiliar terrain. "Both are dark and both are dangerous, one by design and one by chance."

"Lord Montrain and M. Lusignon," Maud murmured eagerly.

"One of these men is to be trusted and one is to be avoided at all costs. One intends to deceive you while the other is your friend. Not only is he your friend, he wishes to be more if you would but let him."

Surely Lord Montrain didn't mean to deceive her. Yet wasn't M. Lusignon her friend? "But which is which? I have to know."

Madame Grimalda shook her head. "If only I could tell you, I would. The future, I've discovered, is a land of mists and shadows, of wraithlike forms, a mysterious expanse dimly seen through a flawed glass. We mustn't complain that our view of the future is clouded. Rather we should marvel that a chosen few were given the gift of catching even an imperfect glimpse of it."

Maud put her hand on the gypsy's silk-clad arm. "You must tell me more," she beseeched.

"Give me your hand once more." Closing her eyes and raising her head to heaven, the gypsy pressed Maud's hand between both of hers. The candle flame wavered uncertainly and dimmed though

Maud felt no breeze. "There is danger waiting for you," Madame Grimalda warned. "Great danger. Very soon. Sooner than you think possible."

Madame Grimalda shuddered. The candle flared brightly. The gypsy opened her eyes and released Maud's hand. "There is no more I can tell you," she said.

Maud rose uncertainly to her feet and stumbled to the tent flap. Looking back, she saw Madame Grimalda, seemingly oblivious, staring at the flickering flame of the candle.

Once outside, the bright sun blinded her. She blinked as the fortuneteller's words reverberated in her mind: "Two dark men. Danger. Sooner than you think."

She opened her eyes and was startled to see Lord Montrain running across the far side of the village green holding something in his upraised hand. Remembering the gypsy's warning, she drew in her breath. No, she couldn't believe he meant her harm.

She frowned, trying to make out what he was doing. Glancing slightly behind and above him, she saw a bobbing orange and black kite trailing a white tail. Yes, he was trying to launch a kite into the air! How strange.

A breeze tugged at her bonnet, the same breeze lifted the kite. Now she noticed the leaves in the trees fluttering in the wind, saw storm clouds massing above the church steeple. When she glanced back at Lord Montrain, he'd stopped running to look up at the kite as it rose in a series of dips and soarings above the tops of the trees.

Lord Montrain walked across the green and handed the stick with the kite's twine wrapped

213

around it to a small tow-haired boy. Grinning, the boy gripped the stick with both hands, slowly unwinding the twine as he watched his kite rise still higher into the sky. Lord Montrain tousled the lad's hair.

Maud smiled fondly. How could a man who helped a boy launch his kite practice deceit? The gypsy's warning must surely refer to M. Lusignon.

A hand touched her arm. She started. "All three of us have been looking for you," her father said. "We must hurry. The rope dancer is about to begin."

Willoughby, "the world's premier rope dancer," performed wondrous feats, executing daring somersaults on the high rope, juggling an orange, a ball, and a ninepin on the inclined rope, and swinging recklessly from side to side while balanced on the slack rope. Maud, however, could only stare at him, unseeing.

"Two men. Danger. Soon."

"Did you say something?" her father asked as they left the rope dancer's tent.

She shook her head.

Taking his watch from his pocket, Lord Ashley said, "We'll be just in time for M. Lusignon's exhibition."

They found a crowd of the curious gathered around a roped-off circle on the green near the church cemetery. M. Lusignon, dressed in black as he had been on the day of his arrival at Twin Oaks, ignored the spectators as he waited with his arms folded. Two men, also in black, stood near him. One had a scar slashing across his cheek; the other's face had been pitted by the smallpox.

"Those two joined Lusignon at Twin Oaks late last night," Lord Ashley whispered. "I can't say I care for either of them. To my mind they're a villainous-looking pair."

The bell in the church steeple tolled the hour.

One of M. Lusignon's companions opened a long black box, removed a rapier, and handed it to him. Striding to the center of the circle, M. Lusignon waited for quiet, then said, "English gentlemen and their ladies, my name is Maurice Lusignon, and I intend to present for your edification a demonstration of the ancient art of fencing."

Maud noted that she as well as everyone near her had to listen carefully to understand his accented words. She smiled to herself, knowing he was perfectly capable of speaking near-perfect English.

"The first fencing schools," the Frenchman went on, "were conducted in ancient Rome to train the gladiators. In the more than eight hundred years since that time, the art of fencing has been associated with combat between individuals — the duel, and combat between nations — war.

"The best fencing schools are usually found where the most battles have recently been fought, and so today they are in Italy, Spain, and in my own native land, France. I must admit, however, that one of the greatest of all fencing masters was English, the magnificent Angelo."

He nodded to his companion with the scarred face. "René," he said, "will now assist me in a brief demonstration of fencing with rapiers. During the Middle Ages when warriors protected their bodies with suits of armor, the heavy two-handed sword was the favorite weapon. Today, fencers use the ra-

215

pier. After my companions and I have finished, you English gentlemen"—he swept his rapier around the circle—"will be given the opportunity to challenge me." He smiled. "If any of you so desire."

René selected a rapier and took his position facing M. Lusignon at a distance of fifteen feet. The third Frenchman took two wire mesh masks and placed one on the ground near each of the fencers.

"En garde!" M. Lusignon called to René.

Looking past the Frenchmen, Maud noticed that Lord Montrain and Philip Faurot had joined the rear ranks of the spectators. Her gaze clung to the frowning Montrain until M. Lusignon spoke again.

"To begin," he said, "the fencer salutes his opponent." He raised his rapier, brought it down smartly, put on his mask, moved his right foot forward, raised his left hand head high and bent it slightly. René did the same.

"Now," Lusignon said, "I show you the lunge." He thrust the rapier forward as he advanced his right foot and straightened his left leg.

Philip Faurot, Maud saw, had edged through the crowd to the rope barrier.

M. Lusignon proceeded to demonstrate the attack, the parry, and the riposte. Removing his mask, he said, "Now, do any of you brave gentlemen wish to test your skill?" When no one stepped forward, he raised an eyebrow. "Certainly there must be one among you. No harm will befall you. You have my word."

A burly farmer pushed his way through the crowd and ducked under the rope.

"Bien. Select your weapon, my friend."

216

The farmer picked up a rapier, put on a mask and a canvas jacket.

"En garde!"

The farmer saluted awkwardly. After an instant's pause, M. Lusignon leaped forward, feinted, nicked his opponent on the breast of the protective jacket. Startled, the Englishman roared in anger, raised his sword and charged Lusignon, swinging his weapon wildly back and forth. Lusignon countered, steel clashed on steel, and all at once the farmer's rapier sailed through the air and fell harmlessly on the grass. The crowd gasped.

M. Lusignon gave his vanquished foe an ironical bow. *"Merci,"* he told him. He looked around him. "Are there any others?"

Philip Faurot stepped into the circle and faced Lusignon.

"Ah." A look of surprised satisfaction appeared on the Frenchman's face.

Philip accepted a rapier and mask but refused the protection of the canvas jacket. The two men faced each other, Philip looking grimly determined, Lusignon smilingly confident. Maud held her breath as they saluted one another and the duel began.

Lusignon attacked, lunging, feinting, thrusting, as Philip retreated, parrying. Back and forth across the circle they fought, sweat glistening on their faces, steel ringing against steel.

Lusignon thrust, feinted, thrust again. Maud gasped as the tip of his blade slashed Philip's shirt above his breast. Philip retreated once more. Lusignon relentlessly pressed the attack—there was no question in Maud's mind but that he was the better swordsman—and again his rapier slashed across

217

Philip's upper chest, leaving a thin trail of blood.

Desperate, Philip leaped forward. The two men faced each other less than a foot apart with rapiers hilt to hilt until Lusignon sprang back, then thrust. Philip leaped aside, his shirt gaping open, Lusignon's blade having missed him by a hairsbreadth. Did Lusignon mean to kill him? Maud opened her mouth to cry a warning.

Montrain ducked under the rope and strode into the circle, ignoring the flashing steel as he separated the two men. "Enough," he said.

Lusignon, his chest heaving, stepped back and lowered his rapier.

Montrain grasped Philip's arm and led his protesting friend away but not before Maud had seen the scar in the form of an X on his blood-smeared bared right shoulder. She gasped, for here was proof positive that he was an imposter. He wasn't Philip Faurot; he was Guy Gournay.

Chapter Fifteen

When Maud was a young girl and living at Twin Oaks during the summer, she looked forward to storms. She waited until the rain stopped and then hastened to the far corner of the garden where there was a knoll with a gully starting near its crest and ending half a mile away at the brook. Though usually dry, for several hours following a heavy rain a stream of water flowed down this gully.

Maud would use rocks and dirt to block this run off, watching the water rise higher and higher until at last a rift appeared in her dam. Suddenly the water would burst through the ever-widening opening and rush in a miniature torrent to the brook.

When M. Lusignon's rapier bared the scar on Philip Faurot's shoulder at the Ashton Fair, it seemed to Maud that another kind of dam had burst. Event now followed event with dizzying speed.

A few minutes after Maud, her father, Gwen, and Mrs. Wilcomb returned to Twin Oaks from the fair, Philip Faurot—Maud still didn't think of him as Guy Gournay—galloped up the driveway and sprang from his horse. After striding into the house, he was closeted with Lord Ashley for half an hour before riding away. He left Twin Oaks, she noted, not by way of the London road but along the track leading past the monastery.

She saw M. Lusignon and his two companions arrive soon after Philip left. René hurried to the stable and, minutes later, rode back toward the road. M. Lusignon roamed the lower hallways of the house, his hands clasped behind his back, his bowed head belying the darting watchfulness of his eyes. The third Frenchman — Auguste — wandered about the grounds, now and again cocking his head to listen when thunder rumbled in the distance.

To revive her flagging spirits, Maud had Agnes help her change into a gown of forget-me-not blue silk with white lace framing the low scoop of the décolletage, the tiered skirt trimmed with royal blue braid and lace. She put on a three-strand pearl necklace, pearl drop earrings, and tied a royal blue ribbon in her hair. She thought of the gown, one of her favorites, as a talisman that would bring good fortune. If anything could.

After a dinner at which only Lord Ashley and M. Lusignon seemed to have their normal appetites, Maud sought refuge in the library. Hearing hoof-beats and the rattle of a carriage, she hurried to one of the high narrow windows, gasping with surprise when she saw Lord Montrain drive his curricle to the front entrance. Her sudden surge of hope was dashed a moment later when Gwen ran outside to meet him and, together, they disappeared into the house.

She turned from the window. Holding back tears, she climbed the ladder and removed the fourth volume of *Decline and Fall* from the topmost shelf. Walking slowly to the fireplace, almost as though mesmerized, she let the book fall open in her hands to the daisies she'd so carefully pressed between its pages.

She stared wistfully at the now dry and fragile flower tiara, recalling the day—it seemed so long ago!—when she'd placed it there. How happy she'd been then, how full of great expectations. Even now she couldn't bring herself to brush the forlorn flowers into the grate.

"Maud." The word was little more than a whisper.

She turned. Gwen stood in the doorway with Lord Montrain hovering uncomfortably behind her in the hall.

Gwen stared at her, hurried to her, stopped an arm's length away, and then glanced behind her. Lord Montrain answered her silent bidding by stepping into the room. When Gwen continued to look at him, he crossed the library to stand behind her.

Once more Gwen turned to Maud, putting her hand lightly on her arm. "John and I are on our way to Gretna Green," she said. "We leave tonight. Now."

Maud's head jerked back; the book fell, thudding on the floor. Bile rose to her throat and the room whirled around her. She had to grasp the edge of the mantel to steady herself.

Gwen took her hand. "Are you all right?" she asked.

"Don't touch me." Maud shrank away. She tried to speak, failed, drew a series of deep breaths.

221

"Yes, I'm all right," she managed to say. "Startled. Not surprised. No, not surprised in the least."

Why was Lord Montrain kneeling? Then she saw that the book she'd dropped had fallen open and the daisy circlet had shattered, the pieces scattering over the red carpet. He carefully returned each fragment to its place between the pages, looking at the recreated crown for a long moment before gently closing the book and handing it to her. His eyes refused to meet hers.

"Thank you." She was dry-eyed, beyond tears. "You leave tonight," she said, repeating Gwen's words. "So soon." Yet she couldn't help wishing they'd go at once so she could be alone with her grief.

Gwen nodded. "Tonight," she said again.

Vaguely Maud became aware of someone standing in the hall just outside the library door. M. Lusignon? Following her gaze, Gwen glanced behind her, then turned and embraced her sister. Maud stood unmoving, her body rigid, her arms at her sides.

"Maud," Gwen whispered in her ear. "You must help me. You must help us. Do you hear me?"

She nodded.

"You must distract M. Lusignon. This very night. I want you to do all in your power to keep him here at Twin Oaks for as long as possible. Do you understand, Maud? It's desperately important, a matter of life or death."

"Life or death?" she repeated, pitching her voice low. Gwen wasn't usually so melodramatic. What could she mean?

222

"Yes, life or death." Gwen shook her. "Do you hear me, Maud? Do you understand what I've said?"

"Yes. I'm to distract M. Lusignon. I'm to keep him here tonight."

"Always remember," Gwen whispered, "I love you." There were tears in her eyes.

Maud didn't answer. Gwen hugged her quickly, turned to Lord Montrain, and took his arm, urging him from the room. Even so, he hung back, hesitating in the doorway to look at Maud, and for a moment she thought he meant to speak, but he shook his head, turned, and they were gone.

M. Lusignon was no longer in the hallway. If he ever had been.

Moments later she heard Gwen and Lord Montrain's voices at the front of the house, heard the snap of a whip and the rattle of the departing curricle.

An aching numbness settled over her like a shroud. I won't cry, she told herself. Not now. Maybe not ever. Finding that she still held the book in her hand, she turned her back to the window, climbed the ladder, returned it to its place on the top shelf, climbed down again, looked up, and found M. Lusignon standing just inside the door, watching her.

"You're terribly pale," he said.

"They're eloping to Gretna Green. Lord Montrain and my sister." Her voice was a monotone.

"I heard. Rather, I couldn't help overhearing." Even while making this admission of eavesdropping, he lost none of his urbanity.

223

Not answering, she looked around her, knowing that if she didn't sit down or hold onto something she might faint. She gripped the edge of a table.

"I'll send for spirits of ammonia," he said.

She shook her head. "Please don't. I'm all right. My sister's news was sudden though hardly a surprise. I've suspected the truth for weeks and weeks."

He came to her and took her hand, bowing over it with his customary gallantry. "They were cruel."

She stared down at her hand in his, feeling neither comfort nor repugnance, wondering whether she'd ever feel anything again. "No, not cruel," she told him. "You can't force others to do your bidding. No matter how much you might like to."

M. Lusignon reluctantly released her hand. "I can see from looking at you how unhappy you are. I'm most sorry. It always distresses me to see a sorrowing woman, particularly a beautiful woman, and most especially you, Lady Maud."

He glanced across the room and said, "Your pardon," and strode to the window where he opened the sash and spoke to someone. Recalling her promise to Gwen, she stepped to one side so she could look past him and saw Auguste standing outside on the flagstones with two men she recognized as members of M. Lusignon's retinue.

When M. Lusignon turned from the window, Maud said, "An ice. I would like an ice." She desperately needed time to think, to decide what to do.

"I'll ring."

"Shall we walk onto the terrace? I'm certain the fresh air will be good for me. And we'll be able to watch the lightning."

"You're not afraid? Most ladies of my acquaintance, French as well as English, would be." There was a reminiscent look in his eyes. "When I visited my aunt in Provence last year, I found that during lightning storms she sought refuge in the wine cellar of her home. She also quaked at the sound of the thunder. And she avoids fresh air; I believe she suspects it carries the plague."

M. Lusignon, she was reminded, enjoyed nothing more than talking about his experiences. "I'm only afraid of lightning," she said, her thoughts still on Lord Montrain and Gwen rather than thunderstorms, "if it's striking nearby." How could she do as Gwen had asked, she wondered. How could she distract M. Lusignon? She was hardly able to think coherently much less plan.

By the time she finished her ice, though, she'd conceived a dangerous scheme. The risks to herself were great, but what choice did she have? Heartsore as she was, it never occurred to her not to honor Gwen's request even though she didn't understand the reason for it. Gwen had pleaded for her help; that was reason enough.

She rose from her chair, putting her hand to her forehead.

"You have the headache?" M. Lusignon sounded more hopeful than concerned.

"It's nothing. Perhaps I'll feel better if we walk in the garden."

"But what of the coming storm?"

The setting sun, she saw, was hidden by dark clouds. Lightning danced in the distance along the horizon, the flickerings followed by rolls of thunder.

She'd seen similar lightning earlier in the week, but no rain had fallen. "Heat lightning," Mrs. Wilcomb had called it.

"We won't walk far," she promised. "Only to the grotto."

M. Lusignon frowned, so Maud said, "Let me tell Sproul where we'll be in case anyone asks."

When she returned to the terrace, M. Lusignon smiled, bowed, and offered her his arm. "I have never visited your grotto," he said, "but it has the sound of a place intended for a romantic rendezvous."

She lowered her head, feigning embarrassment at the same time she tried to conceal her nervousness. "I was impressed by your fencing exhibition," she said as though to change the subject. This was true; never before had she seen such skill with a rapier. She must, she told herself, be as truthful as possible.

"I fear my mentor wouldn't have shared your enthusiasm if he had been at the Ashton Fair to observe me. He would say my attack showed how much I have neglected to practice. Did I make mention of the fact that I learned the art of fencing from Pierre Vallee himself? I hope you don't think me immodest when I tell you M. Vallee often said I was his most promising pupil. In fact, he desired me to remain with him at his Paris academy as his protégé so I might eventually take his place."

"I found the way you humbled Guy Gournay nothing less than incredible."

"I cannot accept your plaudits since Gournay is a mere amateur. But don't let us speak of him. In time I shall have my revenge on M. Gournay. That is all I care to say."

They walked through the garden without speaking, the evening darkening as clouds arched higher in the sky. The rumble of thunder grew louder.

"This is the entrance to our grotto," she told him.

They descended three stone steps to a semicircle of lawn enclosed on three sides by high, thick bushes and on the fourth side, in front of them, a hollowed-out hill. Low benches faced a splashing fountain surmounted by a statue of Pan lustily playing his pipes.

"Charming." M. Lusignon covered Maud's hand with his as he spoke as though to tell her he referred to her as well as to the grotto. He led her to one of the benches where he sat at her side in the deepening twilight.

"Your headache?" he asked.

"No better." When she saw him reach for his watch, she quickly said, "You once told me how you learned Herr Mesmer's methods from your father, but you've said little about the cures you've achieved."

She held her breath as he patted his watch pocket, sighing with relief when he raised his hand to his mustache in a preening gesture.

"Ah, yes," he said. "I have to admit I've accomplished a great deal. Years ago, in ought-one or ought-two, I was living temporarily in a pension in Gstaad when I learned that the daughter of the establishment had suffered the loss of her memory. Not that she failed to know who she was, no, no, nothing quite so dramatic. The young lady had had the misfortune to experience an unhappy love affair and, in a fit of depression, had run away from home.

"Despite an extensive search she wasn't found for more than a fortnight. When I met her some months later, she could remember what occurred before her disappearance and also what happened afterwards but as for the time she was missing— nothing. She could not remember where she had gone or what she had done."

"And you cured her?"

"I'm gratified to be able to tell you I did. After five or six of my treatments, her memory was completely restored."

"And what had she done during those fourteen days?"

M. Lusignon cleared his throat. "Since I considered myself to be the young lady's physician, I fear I'm not at liberty to say. I can tell you, however, that her escapades during that time might make you question the virtue of womankind."

"I realize you wouldn't want me to do that." She let an instant pass before asking, "Have you helped others?"

"There are many who owe M. Lusignon a debt of gratitude. There was a wealthy woman of noble birth from Barcelona, for one, who couldn't resist removing small items from shops without troubling to pay for them; and an English gentleman residing in Nice who, for reasons of health, was attempting to abandon a lifetime's overindulgence in gin."

He went on to describe, in entertaining and exhaustive detail, several of his other successes. With

Gallic shrugs, he also related, briefly, a few of his failures.

Maud listened attentively, offering an appreciative and encouraging comment from time to time. She'd often heard men claim they admired wit in a woman. What they actually meant, she'd concluded, was that a woman should have the wit to listen to *them*. At the moment she didn't mind listening since it postponed the moment she dreaded but knew must come.

A loud peal of thunder climaxed one of M. Lusignon's tales making them both look up at the threatening sky. "We should return to the house," he said.

She put her hand to her head.

"Your malaise is worse?"

"Could you possibly help me? As you did before?"

"Not only will I cure the ache in your head, it may also be in my power to ease the shock of today's unhappy events. Not to banish them from your memory but to place them at what will seem a great distance."

"If you could, I'd be eternally grateful."

"My only wish is to help you in any way I can. You must be aware that from the moment I first saw you, Lady Maud, you've occupied a special niche in my heart."

She turned her head away from him.

"But I realize, of course," he said, "that in your present condition, any words of mine must unfortunately fall on barren soil. I must first cure your malaise." Removing his watch from his pocket, he said, "I'm certain you remember how I asked you to observe the swinging watch."

The dreaded moment was at hand.

"It's become so dark I can hardly see it," she managed to say.

"You're such an excellent subject, my dear Lady Maud, that the darkness need not concern us. Sweep your mind clean of all extraneous material, keep your eye on the watch as best you can, and listen to me."

"I will."

She heard the wind rise, the leaves in the trees rustle, at first from afar and then closer and closer. A gust tugged at her hair.

As he had before, M. Lusignon held his watch aloft, letting it swing like a pendulum while he whispered soothing words, repeating them over and over again like an incantation, his voice gradually fading into silence. After waiting a few moments, he reached out and touched her face and when she didn't respond, murmured, *"Oui,"* as though to himself. He then began to speak to her in English.

What he told her she would desire to do after she awakened would have elicited a shocked gasp from any genteelly brought up young lady and, at the very least, a raised eyebrow from the most worldly of courtesans. Maud gave no sign of any kind.

He clapped his hands. "Awake, my dear," he said. "Awake."

"I am awake."

"And your headache?"

"Headache? I no longer have a headache."

"Très bien."

230

"Nine times seven. Tell me, Maurice, how much is nine times seven?"

"What an odd question." He paused. "Sixty-three."

"Sixty-three, just as I thought."

"Now I have a question for you, Maud. Who is your dearest friend?"

She answered in a low, rotelike voice. "You are, Maurice."

"Would I ever harm you, Maud?"

"Never."

"Tell me what you want of me, Maud."

"I want you to kiss me."

He reached for her, his fingers caressing her cheek, making their way slowly down along her neck, across the strands of pearls to the valley between her breasts in the scoop of her décolletage. She gave no sign of pleasure or displeasure.

All at once she stood and moved away from him. "Not here," she whispered. "Follow me. I know the perfect place." Several large drops of rain struck her face.

"I can hardly see you, Maud." Lightning flashed nearby. "Ah, there you are. The rain begins. Are you leading me to some sheltered spot? A summerhouse? A gazebo, perhaps?"

She ran up the steps from the grotto. "Follow me," she called softly over her shoulder.

"I am following you. Where are you now?"

"Here, Maurice, only a few steps ahead of you. Can't you see me? You must hurry."

"I know how impatient you must be to—" His words were interrupted by his sharp intake of

231

breath. "A branch struck my face," he said.

Again lightning flashed and thunder boomed.

"Maud?" he called.

From her place of concealment behind a tree in what was the thickest grove in the Twin Oak woods, she waited for the next flash of lightning to make certain the roofs and chimneys of the house were out of sight.

"Where are you, my dear Maud? I can't see you."

Once more she waited for the lightning's flash and then, holding her skirts in her hands, walked as quickly and quietly as she could in the direction of the house. The windblown rain stung her face, her hair straggled damply onto her face, her clothes became sodden and heavy.

From far behind her she heard M. Lusignon. "Maud, my dear, where are you?" His plaintive cries grew fainter until they were swallowed up by the bluster of the storm.

When she came to the driveway, she saw a bobbing light ahead of her. When two men approached, she recognized them as Auguste and René. Auguste held up the lantern, and she saw he was hatless with rivulets of rain running down his face onto his water-dark clothes.

"M. Lusignon," Auguste said. "It is most important we find him at once. Have you seen him?"

She nodded.

"Where?" His voice was urgent.

She pointed in the opposite direction from which she'd come, pointed toward the path leading over the hill to the brook and the glen.

"Bien," Auguste said. *"Merci."* Another two

Frenchmen, both carrying lanterns, appeared out of the storm. After a brief discussion, all four hurried away in the direction she'd pointed out.

Once inside the house, she hastened to the stairs.

"Lady Maud." It was Sproul. "I'll call Agnes to help you."

Shaking her head, she told him, "Please don't. I'm all right."

She hurried up the stairs to her room where she stripped off her sodden clothes, dried herself as best she could, put on a nightgown, and threw herself on the bed. Her tears, so long denied, came at last, and she lay sobbing as peals of thunder followed flashes of lightning while the rain beat its mournful tattoo on the slates over her head.

Chapter Sixteen

Maud woke to the glare of morning sunshine and the sound of tapping on her bedchamber door.

Agnes entered in response to her mumbled summons. "Begging your pardon, Lady Maud," her maid said, "but it's that M. Lusignon. He's leaving Twin Oaks and says he must see you afore he goes."

Maud closed her eyes to hold back the tears as she remembered that Gwen had eloped with Lord Montrain. Yesterday her grief had been a piercing pain, keeping her awake until near dawn. Dazed from lack of sleep, she still felt the dull, unremitting ache of Montrain's betrayal. Not wanting to speak to anyone today, especially an angry M. Lusignon, she shook her head.

"He's been waiting for you in the entrance hall for ever so long," Agnes said. "He won't leave until he sees you, or so he says."

Maud's eyes opened wide in surprise.

Agnes lowered her voice. "I'm thinking his lordship would like him and all those other Frenchmen gone. And sooner rather than later."

M. Lusignon probably thought she was cowering in her bedchamber, Maud told herself. That wasn't it at all. She certainly wasn't afraid of him, and she wasn't about to let him think she was. Yes, she'd not only see him, but she'd do so holding her head high.

With Agnes's help, she dressed in a mauve morning gown and hurried to the top of the stairs only to pause there before descending the steps with a deliberate slowness. M. Lusignon, one hand on the newel post at the bottom, looked up at her. She was surprised, though not unpleasantly so, to see that his unsmiling face was crisscrossed with scratches.

He bowed to her, then offered her his hand.

Hesitating only an instant, she took his hand and allowed him to lead her along the hall toward the front door.

"My dear Maud," he said, "I want you to witness the wounded who walk."

She gave him an inquiring look but said nothing. When Sproul opened the door for them, she saw the Frenchman's Napoleon carriage waiting in the drive below.

"Observe Auguste and René, if you please," he told her.

Auguste and two of the other Frenchmen were lashing the last of M. Lusignon's many trunks and portmanteaux to the top of the carriage. René, his right arm bound in a sling, stood on the gravel behind the carriage watching them work. When Auguste came to join him, she noticed he walked with a decided limp.

"The wounded who walk," M. Lusignon said ruefully. "Last night during the thunderstorm both Auguste and René had the misfortune to tumble down a steep hill and fall into your brook. And I myself look like a man who did battle with a wild-cat."

If she told him she was sorry, she'd be lying, so she merely clucked her tongue as Mrs. Wilcomb was wont to do.

"I must confess the greatest injury is not to my body but to my pride. Every morning without fail I admonish myself, 'Maurice, do not underestimate your opponent.' Unfortunately, there comes a time every now and then when I fail to heed my own excellent advice."

He inclined his head toward her in tribute. "You were wonderful, Lady Maud. You wreaked havoc upon my loyal band of followers; in addition, you outdueled me in a battle of wits and by so doing you allowed Guy Gournay more than sufficient time to make his escape to France. I congratulate you."

She repeated his gesture by bowing her head in silent acknowledgement.

"When I attempted to mesmerize you in the grotto," he accused her, "you occupied your mind by repeating the multiplying tables. Is that not true?"

"Only the nine-times table. I always have to concentrate more when I do the nines."

"And when we left Twin Oaks last night you neglected to tell Sproul we were walking to the grotto, did you not?"

"I'm afraid I told him nothing at all."

"And later you sent Auguste and the others to search for me in a place where I was not to be found."

"I admit it. I did all you say I did. You've uncovered every last one of my deceits."

236

"Never have I met such a magnificent woman." He lowered his voice. "I have a dilemma. I must return to France, and yet I cannot bear to leave you. Come with me to Paris, my dear Maud. Escape from this desultory wilderness of Surrey to a civilized city where your beauty and your talents will be appreciated."

Maud stared at him in amazement, not knowing whether she should be insulted or complimented by his indelicate proposal. She decided, instead, to be amused. Smiling, she shook her head. "We aren't confined to Surrey for the entire year," she told him, "since we spend our winters in London."

"London?" He sounded incredulous. "London doesn't compare to Paris. And Londoners admit the truth of what I say by imitating all things French. Isn't it a fact that in the *ton* it's de rigueur to do everything possible *à la Francaise?*"

"That may be true of some."

"My dear Maud," he persisted, "I offer you more than Paris. I'll show you Vienna and Venice and Rome. We'll sail the turquoise seas of the Caribbean, visit the fabled temples of the Orient, travel from the tropical jungles of the Amazon to the snowy steppes of Russia. I offer you the entire world to explore if only you'll permit me to take you away from this." He flung out his arm, so she knew he meant not only Twin Oaks but all it stood for. "This is so dull, so ordinary, so tedious, so prosaic, so tame. This is so—so—"

"So English?"

"Exactly. The very word I sought."

"But M. Lusignon, don't forget I *am* English."

"In this life, each of us must attempt to overcome

237

the limitations that, through no fault of our own, we inherit by the accident of our birth. If you consent to go with me, Lady Maud, I'll change you from an Englishwoman to a citizeness of the world."

"Are you perchance asking me to marry you, M. Lusignon?"

He stared at her as though doubting he'd heard her aright. "Am I asking you to marry me? Was the word *marriage* mentioned? You shock me. I offer you an opportunity that occurs but once in a woman's lifetime, if that often. I offer you exotic adventure. I offer you romance. And what do you do? You speak of their exact opposite, of marriage. Maud, you *are* English."

"And because I am what I was born to be, M. Lusignon, I must refuse your offer."

"You'll discover I'm an extraordinarily patient man, Maud. Though your reply has put me in a state of temporary disarray, I assure you I shall persevere. I believe, in all honesty, we shall one day—"

She heard a footfall behind them. M. Lusignon stopped and turned. "Lord Ashley," he said. "How kind of your lordship to come to bid me farewell."

"I wouldn't have missed the opportunity for the world," Lord Ashley said with evident sincerity. "You're on your way home to France?"

"I am. I cannot express how much I appreciated your wonderful hospitality." He looked at Maud. "If you are ever in Paris, remember that M. Maurice Lusignon is at your service. Yours too, of course, Lord Ashley."

He shook hands with his host; he kissed Maud's hand. As he climbed into the coach, he turned to

Maud. "By the way," he told her, "I consider it my duty to inform you I never had a sister."

No sister? No Angelique? She frowned. That meant no one had been driven to suicide after her love was spurned by Guy Gournay. M. Lusignon had evidently lied to her about the reason for his hatred of his fellow countryman. Well, she thought, knowing M. Lusignon as well as she did, she shouldn't be surprised.

After Auguste was helped to mount a gray gelding, he rode ahead of the carriage as an outrider. The coachman's whip cracked above the horses, and the carriage started off. M. Lusignon leaned from the window. *"Adieu,"* he called, waving his hat. "Maud, I believe we shall one day meet again. *Adieu, adieu."*

The carriage rounded the sweep of the drive, passed under the two oaks, and disappeared into the woods.

"I can't in all honesty say I'm sorry to see the last of them," Lord Ashley said. "M. Lusignon is definitely not my cup of tea."

"I think he would be quick to inform you that a glass of sparkling French champagne is not intended to be anyone's cup of tea."

Lord Ashley scowled. "I dare say *I* wouldn't compare him to champagne, sparkling or otherwise. Is it possible you were taken with the man, Maud?"

"I didn't like him, Papa, and I certainly didn't trust him. He lied, he was devious, and he sought to take every advantage whether by fair means or foul." A reminiscent look came into her eyes. "On the other hand, I will say this for M. Lusignon.

Whenever I was with him I felt as though I were a woman."

"Harrumph," was her father's only comment. With a sweep of his hand, he invited Maud back into the house. "Shall we go to the drawing room?" he asked. "I have a few matters of considerable importance to discuss with you."

She glanced a question at him, but he continued to look straight ahead.

"I confess I don't have a glimmering of what Lusignon meant," Lord Ashley said, "when he told you he had no sister, but I learned yesterday that he's not completely without a family. Did you know he has a wife and five children living in Paris?"

She raised her eyebrows. "I didn't know, but I don't suppose I'm too surprised. I also expect he keeps a mistress."

"*That* is a matter about which a young lady shouldn't concern herself."

She wanted to say, "Yet I'm forced to be at least mildly interested when only a few minutes ago I was invited to be mistress number two." Not wanting to see her father overset, she let the matter drop.

In the drawing room, Lord Ashley settled himself in the center of a comfortably upholstered sofa near the fireplace while Maud perched expectantly on the edge of one of the high-backed chairs.

"After we returned from the Ashton Fair yesterday," he began, "I had a most surprising conversation with Mr. Philip Faurot in the course of which he extracted a promise from me to reveal nothing of our discussion until M. Lusignon had left Twin Oaks. I say Mr. Faurot, but that isn't completely accurate since the first thing he told me was that he was not Mr. Faurot at all but Guy Gournay, the duc de Carteret or however these Frenchmen style themselves."

A duke! Maud thought. He hadn't acted like a duke. Or had he? She recalled how everyone had remarked that Lord Montrain deferred to him.

"M. Lusignon," she said, "told me he came here because he suspected our Mr. Faurot was actually a Frenchman named Guy Gournay. He claimed Guy Gournay was the cause of his sister Angelique killing herself, but since he has no sister, he was obviously lying."

"Ah, that explains his mention of the nonexistence of a sister." He shook his head as though to show how much he regretted the flawed characters of men in general and M. Lusignon in particular. "We've heard a great many misstatements of late. Most of which, if not all, emanated from Frenchmen. I suppose I shouldn't be surprised." He glanced at the window in the direction M. Lusignon and his retinue had gone. "They're a clumsy lot as well. Did you notice one of them had his arm in a sling, another limped, and Lusignon himself looked like he'd fallen head foremost into a briar patch?"

Maud suppressed a smile. "M. Lusignon didn't lie about everything," she said. "He did hate Guy Gournay. I quite feared he might kill him at the Ashton Fair."

"Gournay told me why," Lord Ashley said. "It's a deuce of a coil, but let me see if I can unravel it for you. The elder Gournays, he told me—and other information I've received leads me to believe him—were émigrés who fled France years ago, after the Revolution, traveling to America where they assumed new identities. In short, they became Faurots.

"Now that Napoleon's in exile and the Bourbons have been restored to the French throne, the Gournay lands have been returned to them. Several months ago, the old duke died in New Orleans after a lengthy illness, and Guy, his only heir, left America for his homeland, accompanied by his friend, Montrain. Since the Gournays have democratic ideas, reinforced by their lengthy stay in America, a powerful reactionary faction in France sought to prevent Guy from regaining his inheritance and later, perhaps, changing the course of French history."

"And M. Lusignon was their agent."

"Exactly. Chosen because of friends in high places here in England. Once Guy returns to France, where the Gournays are immensely popular with their people, he'll be safe. So Lusignon sought to find him and prevent his return. By killing him if need be."

Maud shuddered. "How horrible." After a moment's reflection, she frowned. "If Guy Gournay would be safe in France, why did he tarry here in Surrey?"

"Hah! What prompts a Frenchman, young or old, to do anything? Love, of course."

"Love?" Totally confused, she could only stare at her father.

"The reason Guy Gournay was so anxious to speak to me last night," Lord Ashley said, "was to ask for your sister's hand in marriage. It seems she'd delayed and delayed her answer, finally accepting him yesterday at the Ashton Fair, of all places. After her infatuations with Georgie Plimsall and all the others, on this occasion she wisely waited until she was certain she was truly in love."

Maud couldn't credit what she'd heard. "Gwen and Guy Gournay? Surely you're mistaken, Papa."

"I believe you must be familiar with Dr. Johnson's remark: 'Sir, when a man knows he is to be hanged in a fortnight, it concentrates his mind wonderfully.' Now I freely admit I often attach a wrong name to a man or fail to hear a man's name correctly above the hubbub at the tables at Watier's. When a man asks for my daughter's hand, however, it does serve to concentrate my mind enough so I'm able to recall his name a day later."

"Don't tease me, Papa!"

"I swear to you it was Guy Gournay and no other. I reluctantly gave my consent—he may be a duke, but he's French, after all—and he and your sister departed last evening for his estate in the south of France."

Her head whirled. Gwen and Guy Gournay. Which meant she hadn't eloped to Gretna Green with Lord Montrain. Gwen had lied to her. Why? To deceive M. Lusignon? Quite probably.

"I've always thought of Frenchmen," her father said, "as peacocks, proud of their colorful plumage, given to emitting shrill cries but lacking substance. This Gournay appears a decent chap, though."

"I wonder if you'd approve of anyone Gwen chose to marry."

"A father is always at a disadvantage when judging son-in-laws since he's forced to compare them with someone of better character and superior abilities. Namely himself."

As her father rambled on, she felt a strange inter-mingling of emotions. Relief and joy because Gwen and Montrain weren't in love and never harbored any intentions of marrying, confusion as to what had actually happened and why, and anger over be-ing lied to. She'd need time sort out her conflicting feelings, time to put the pieces of the puzzle to-gether, if she ever could. First she must ask her father about Lord Montrain.

"—but expect to return to Twin Oaks before the start of the shooting season on the first of Septem-ber," she heard him say.

"I'm sorry but I must have missed something," she told him.

"I said I leave next Tuesday to spend a week at Sheffields where one of the guests will be Marianne Comfort, the widow of Joshua Comfort who had the misfortune to suffer a fatal fall from his horse two years ago. I've always found Mrs. Comfort to be attractive, unaffected, and accomplished. All in all a most agreeable woman."

Maud had always liked Mrs. Comfort. She was not only most agreeable, she recalled, she had other virtues as well, being handsome for an older woman of forty-odd and reportedly having an annual in-come in the neighborhood of five thousand pounds.

Since she'd never heard her father speak so favor-ably of any other woman, it struck her that he must have a reason. "Are you thinking of asking for her hand in marriage?" she wondered.

"Only time will tell." She noticed a glint in his eyes that suggested he'd already made up his mind. "Would you have any objection if I did, Maud?"

"No, no, of course not. In any event, you don't

have to ask my permission."

Her father glanced at the portrait of his wife above the fireplace. "I've often told you how much you remind me of your mother. I expect it wasn't your permission I was asking for, it was hers."

Maud reached out and covered her father's hand with her own. "She'd have no objection, of that I'm certain."

Her father put his other hand to his face. He closed his eyes, and she knew his thoughts had journeyed into the past. His lips trembled, and for a moment she thought he was about to sob. He did not, however; he drew a deep breath, sighed, and took her hand between both of his.

"Thank you, Maud," he said.

She felt closer to her father than she ever had before. But she could restrain her curiosity no longer. "Lord Montrain," she said. "I saw him here at Twin Oaks with Gwen last evening. Where is he now?"

"Blackstone House stands empty," her father said. "Lord Montrain has left England with Gwen and Guy Gournay. By now I expect he's either in mid-Channel or somewhere in the south of France."

Chapter Seventeen

When she left her father, Maud went to the library where she gazed dispiritedly at the forlorn shreds of the daisy circlet pressed between the pages of *Decline and Fall*. Her heart, she thought, was as shattered as the flowers. Would it ever be whole again?

After returning the book to the shelf, she walked to the stable to exercise Ne'er-Do-Well only to discover that Tom had already put the horse through his morning regimen.

She wandered listlessly into the garden, finally taking a path leading away from the house. On any other occasion she would have savored the delightful summer day—the storm of the night before had ended the long spell of hot weather, and now a cool morning breeze caressed her face while overhead the deep blue of the sky was punctuated by windblown cotton puffs of clouds. Today, however, she was oblivious to her surroundings.

Since her father had been able to tell her nothing further concerning Lord Montrain, questions whirled about in her mind. If Gwen and Guy Gournay were to be married, and there seemed no doubt of it, Montrain's interest in her sister had evidently been a ruse, a ruse known to both Gwen and Gournay.

If so, why had Montrain bothered to stage the charade of abducting her from Twin Oaks? Afterwards, why hadn't he told her the truth instead of attempting to deceive her by piling falsehood on top of falsehood to create a tottering structure doomed to fall?

Perhaps he'd believed she couldn't be trusted with an important secret. If so, he'd sorely misjudged her. Another explanation occurred to her — was it possible he lacked all feeling for others, seeing his deception as nothing more than an amusing ploy in a game of hearts?

No! He was an honorable man. She couldn't believe she could have so mistaken his character. There must be an explanation for his actions, probably a simple and satisfying one, though she couldn't think what it might be. Still, such a reason might exist, but, if so, why hadn't he told her what it was long ago? He certainly hadn't lacked for opportunities. He could have confided in her when he found her alone at the monastery ruins, when she visited Blackstone House with Mrs. Wilcomb, when they met at the Newmarket races or at the Ashton Fair.

No matter what his reason for deceiving her might have been, if he'd intended to leave Twin Oaks with Guy Gournay and never return, he would have left a message for her. A gentleman, and he *was* a gentleman in the fullest sense of the word, could do no less.

She stopped, her eyes opening wide as she held this thought to her as a drowning woman might clutch a piece of floating debris. He hadn't left a message. Therefore, without the slightest doubt, he meant to return to Twin Oaks. She nodded hopefully, pleased with this optimistic conclusion.

Looking about her, she realized she'd been walking in a daze. Without conscious intent, she'd followed the path to the brook and now found herself at the top of the wooded slope above the glen.

With her spirits at least momentarily revived, she descended into the glen and crossed the brook by stepping from rock to rock. She sat on the moss-covered knoll near the very spot where, months before—it seemed years—Lord Montrain had watched her swing across the brook on a vine. She gazed wistfully at the vine, knowing she'd never swing on it again. Such hoydenish acts were for girls, and she was a young lady now.

Comforted by the seclusion of the glen and lulled by the murmur of the water, she closed her eyes, letting her fancy roam . . .

She looked up and gasped. Lord Montrain stood at the top of the path leading into the glen. As she watched in startled surprise, he strode down the hill to the brook, waded through the water and climbed the knoll to kneel at her feet.

"It is too much," he said. "I have fought against it and fought against it but to no avail. I cannot help myself. I surrender. The bond between us is too strong for me to break. What began as sport has somehow become my fate. Will you, my dearest Maud, do me the honor of becoming my wife?"

She stared at him. He'd deceived her, and now, in this backhanded, Mr. Darcy-like way, he was asking her to marry him.

"No," she told him, "we will never be suited, you and I. You compliment me by offering for my hand, but I must refuse you."

His eyes opened wide in amazement. "You — you —" he stammered. "You refuse me?"

"If ever any actions of mine may have led you to believe I might be amenable to such a proposal from you, those actions were inadvertent. I intend never to marry, Lord Montrain. Never . . ."

Maud opened her eyes and the scene faded. She glanced around her, aware her imaginings had been invaded by a discordant sound. Hoofbeats? A man's voice?

She looked up and gasped. Lord Montrain stood at the top of the path leading into the glen. How extraordinary! Never before had one of her daydreams ever become real, much less after the passage of mere minutes.

As she watched in startled surprise, he strode down the hill to the brook, crossing the rushing water by carefully stepping from rock to rock, evidently aware that ardor was seldom enhanced by wet feet.

Climbing the knoll, he held out his arms to her. Without hesitation she stood, trying to catch her breath, trying to quell the wild beating of her heart, and ran to him. He gathered her into his arms; he kissed her. Clinging to him, she returned his kiss. Never before had she known such bliss.

He held her away from him. "Darling Maud," he said, "I love you more than I can ever tell you. Will you be my wife?" She wanted to laugh, she wanted to cry. "Oh, yes," she told him, "yes, yes, yes."

Once more he kissed her. And several more times after that, each kiss more wonderfully unsettling than the last. Finally he took her hand and drew her down beside him to sit on the moss.

"Maud, Maud," he said, "have I ever told you how much I like your name? Our first daughter will be named Maud. I insist on it."

She nodded. Of late she'd come to like the name herself, especially on his lips. Once she'd thought it plain. Now she saw it as simple and unaffected.

"Have you no questions?" he asked. "Don't you want to know why I acted in such a disgraceful manner?"

Still pleasantly disoriented by his kisses, it took her a moment to order her thoughts. "I know you must have had compelling reasons for whatever you did."

He raised her hand to his lips and kissed her fingers. "Nevertheless, I intend to tell you everything and then plead for your forgiveness."

How quickly she'd dismissed the questions that only moments before had plagued her! She was ready to put the past behind her, for it was her nature to look to the future even though her natural curiosity remained.

"I've already forgiven you, John," she said, tasting the sound of his given name and finding it delicious.

"I intend to lay any possible doubts to rest." He put his arm around her, drawing her close to him. "It all began," he told her, "because I was beholden to Guy Gournay, who twice saved my life in America, as I once told you. While accompanying him on his journey home to France, we stopped in London so he could confer with other émigrés. While there Guy fell hopelessly in love with your sister."

"She never told me."

"Possibly because at first she didn't realize the depth of her feelings. Or was afraid to acknowledge them. When she vacillated, Guy pursued her, behaving like a man possessed of a demon, even demanding I bring him to Blackstone House so he could be near her. Unfortunately he had to court her in secret to protect her; if his enemies, M. Lusignon in particular, became aware of his interest in Gwen, she would have been in danger. Lusignon wouldn't have hesitated to strike at Guy through her."

"It was natural for Guy to protect Gwen," she said, "but I still don't understand why you attempted to abduct her. You claimed at the time you wanted to bring yourself to her attention."

"I never wanted to abduct Gwen, nor did Guy. In fact, Guy was at Twin Oaks that night for a rendezvous with your sister while I kept watch. We were starting back to Blackstone House when I saw you walking in the fog and gave in to my impulse to carry you off. I admit I acted rashly—Guy was appalled and furious that I asked him to do the actual deed. In my defense I must tell you I couldn't help myself. Desperately as I wanted you, I certainly meant you no harm." He smiled, remembering. "I think I told you at the time that you were the wrong girl. You weren't. You were the right girl; you always have been."

His words were like the sun breaking through dark clouds, bringing a brightness and warmth that made her glow with happiness. "I wish you had told me the truth then."

"I wanted to. I almost did on the day when you came to Blackstone House with Mrs. Wilcomb, but Guy feared you'd inadvertently reveal his secret and in so doing put your sister in jeopardy. 'Wait,' he advised me. 'No harm can come from delay.'

"I understood Guy's fears," he went on. "Though I knew you were capable of keeping a secret, I feared your all-too-revealing expression might give it away. So I put off telling you until now. Last night I left Guy and Gwen safely on a ship bound for France and hastened back to bare my heart to you. Your sister, by the way, sends her love and promises to write as soon as she's settled."

Maud smiled, certain that if her face was so revealing, her love for him must be obvious. "I knew all along you had a good reason for everything you did. My heart told me to trust you. John, I do believe I've loved you ever since that evening when you carried me off."

"I think I've always loved you, Maud. I've spent my entire life looking for you." He drew her close. "We'll marry as soon as possible and then journey to Cornwall."

"Will we live there? It *is* quite far."

"We'll live wherever you please."

"Blackstone House is near both town and Twin Oaks."

"Then Blackstone House it will be."

She gazed at him thoughtfully. "Since the house

252

and gardens are badly in need of attention, I expect I'll be kept busy putting both in order. Old Cob surely doesn't want to live where he's not wanted, so why don't we ask him to come to live at our stables so he can help train Ne'er-Do-Well? Vulcan, too, of course. And Mrs. Wilcomb has always wanted a home of her own. We could ask her if she'd like to have the gatehouse all to herself." She hesitated. "If you're amenable, John."

As he nestled his face in the softness of her hair, the thought came to him, as it must eventually come to all men in similar circumstances, that marriage might not be as simple as he'd imagined. He realized that this stranger, this woman with whom he would share the rest of his life, harbored rather definite ideas, ideas that might not always coincide with his, even though in this case they did.

"Of course I'm amenable," he said.

His long hesitation before answering gave time for her thoughts to stray to subjects surprisingly similar to those that had passed through his mind, namely the momentous changes to be wrought by marriage. When she spoke, though, she didn't address the matter directly but, as is the wont of most women, approached it obliquely.

"I remember," she said, "how angry Gwen became when the tales she read always ended with either the heroine's wedding or her betrothal. She maintained this came about because the intriguing portion of a woman's life, for the most part, ended with her marriage. Gwen even suggested that stories shouldn't conclude with a period and the word *Finis* but should end in mid-sentence to demonstrate that

253

the heroine's story was by no means over."

He smiled for he immediately understood that she was asking for his reassurance. Rising, he reached down, took both her hands in his, and drew her up to stand beside him. "For us," he promised, "marriage will be a beginning, not an ending."

He led her to the hanging vine. "Ever since I saw you swinging across the brook," he said, "there's something I've wanted to do."

Taking her in his arms, he kissed her tenderly. "Hold fast to me," he said as he reached up to grasp the vine with both hands.

She drew in her breath. "The vine won't hold both of us," she protested. "The last time I swung on it I could feel it loosen."

"The vine will carry us safely across the brook to the other side," he promised. "I see it as an omen, Maud, that together we can do as much or even more as we did apart."

She looked down at the brook. "If the vine breaks, we'll land in the pool."

"Are you afraid?"

She shook her head. "As long as I'm with you, John, I'll never fear what the future might hold for me." She corrected herself. "For us."

"Nor will I."

He tightened his grip on the vine while she wrapped her arms around his neck. Running, he leaped from the knoll. Together they swung out over the pool, and then . . .

A Memorable Collection of Regency Romances

BY ANTHEA MALCOLM AND VALERIE KING

LET ARCHER AND CLEARY
AWAKEN AND CAPTURE YOUR HEART!

CAPTIVE DESIRE   (2612, $3.75)
by Jane Archer

Victoria Malone fancied herself a great adventuress and student of life, but being kidnapped by handsome Cord Cordova was too much excitement for even her! Convincing her kidnapper that she had been an innocent bystander when the stagecoach was robbed was futile when he was kissing her until she was senseless!

REBEL SEDUCTION   (3249, $4.25)
by Jane Archer

"Stop that train!" came Lacey Whitmore's terrified warning as she rushed toward the locomotive that carried wounded Confederates and her own beloved father. But no one paid heed, least of all the Union spy Clint McCullough, who pinned her to the ground as the train suddenly exploded into flames.

DREAM'S DESIRE   (3093, $4.50)
by Gwen Cleary

Desperate to escape an arranged marriage, Antonia Winston y Ortega fled her father's hacienda to the arms of the arrogant Captain Domino. She would spend the night with him and would be free for no gentleman wants a ruined bride. And ruined she would be, for Tonia would never forget his searing kisses!

VICTORIA'S ECSTASY   (2906, $4.25)
by Gwen Cleary

Proud Victoria Torrington was short of cash to run her shipping empire, so she traveled to America to meet her partner for the first time. Expecting a withered, ancient cowhand, Victoria didn't know what to do when she met virile, muscular Judge Colston and her body budded with desire.

Available wherever paperbacks are sold, or order direct from the Publisher. Send cover price plus 50¢ per copy for mailing and handling to Zebra Books, Dept. 3758, 475 Park Avenue South, New York, N.Y. 10016. Residents of New York and Tennessee must include sales tax. DO NOT SEND CASH. For a free Zebra/ Pinnacle catalog please write to the above address.